TORCHWOOD

INTO THE
SILENCE

Recent titles in the *Torchwood* series from BBC Books:

TORCHWOOD

INTO THE SILENCE

Sarah Pinborough

2 4 6 8 10 9 7 5 3 1

Published in 2009 by BBC Books, an imprint of Ebury Publishing
A Random House Group company

Torchwood is a BBC Wales production for BBC One
Executive Producers: Russell T Davies and Julie Gardner

The Random House Group Limited Reg. No. 954009.
Addresses for companies within the Random House Group can be found at
www.randomhouse.co.uk

A CIP catalogue record for this book is available from the British Library.

ISBN 978 1 849 90655 5

The Random House Group Limited supports The Forest Stewardship
Council® (FSC®), the leading international forest-certification organisation.
Our books carrying the FSC label are printed on FSC®-certified paper.
FSC is the only forest-certification scheme supported by the leading
environmental organisations, including Greenpeace. Our
paper procurement policy can be found at
www.randomhouse.co.uk/environment

Commissioning Editor: Albert DePetrillo
Series Editor: Steve Tribe
Production Controller: Phil Spencer

Cover design by Lee Binding @ Tea Lady © BBC 2009
Typeset in Albertina and Century Gothic
Printed in Great Britain by Clays Ltd, St Ives plc

*For the S.S.C.C.,
without whom I wouldn't have such great
and ridiculous friends. Stony Stratford rocks!*

Heavy raindrops pattered insistently against the window, searching out a way to creep in. Watching from her bed on the other side of the room, six-year-old Kate Healey pulled the covers up a little further until they stopped just under her nose. Her eyes were wide and her breathing fast. It was only rain, she *knew* that, but, lying there in the dark with her parents all the way downstairs, she thought the drops sounded just like the hungry fingers of dead children tapping at the glass, wanting to get at her warm skin.

Sleep. She had to try to get to sleep because Shona at school said the monsters didn't come for you if you were asleep, and more than anything Kate wanted the monsters to leave her alone. For a moment she let her eyes drift shut, and when she opened them again she was relieved that there were no shapes moving in the shadows of her room. No dead children inside. Or monsters. Or maybe dead children were monsters. Everything was a monster in the dark.

Shivering slightly, Kate wished she didn't have such a *vivid and overactive imagination*. She wasn't entirely sure what the phrase meant, but she knew that whatever it was it made her afraid of stuff that people like her parents didn't even think about. Monsters. Dead people. The bad things that lived in the secret black country under her bed and came out at night. She'd seen her mum and dad both shake their heads and blame her *vivid* or *overactive* imagination for waking them up at night when they had to be at work early. But she couldn't help it, however much she wished differently. And how could she explain that the world *changed* in the dark? And it terrified her.

Outside, the wind became distracted and carried the rain in a different direction, giving the small terraced house's windows some peace. Kate let out a sigh, and her heart slowed slightly to somewhere nearer a normal pace. The dead fingers were gone, at least for now. If only she could *see* to the other side of the room, then bedtime would be so much easier. She peered at the empty space on her bedside table where her night light had been.

Big girls don't sleep with a light on. That's what Daddy had said when he threw it away, despite all her tears. She'd almost gone and fished it out of the bin when no one was looking, but Daddy could be really scary when he was angry and so she'd left it where it was until the rubbish men came and took it away for good. Daddy had thrown it out four days ago, and Kate hadn't slept properly since. It was too dark. Bad things came alive in the dark.

Pulling Lucky the stuffed sheepdog into a tighter hug, she curled her knees up under him and towards her chin. Despite her sockets starting to itch with tiredness, she couldn't bring herself to shut her eyes for more than a moment, knowing that as soon as she did all the shadows in her small room would pull themselves together into something fluid and ancient, intent on creeping up to suffocate her. She blinked. It was a fast movement, too quick for the shadows to act.

From downstairs, the theme tune for some TV detective show that her mum was fond of drifted up towards her, reminding Kate that her bedroom was not a dark universe on its own but was attached to the rest of the warm and brightly lit house. It was a slightly comforting thought and, as the loud music faded into dialogue that she couldn't hear, Kate concentrated instead on the sounds from outside: not the rain, *the dead children's fingers*, but the real-life human sounds of nine o'clock on a Tuesday evening in Cardiff. She was a *big girl*. She'd show them she didn't need a night light.

A train rattled by on the tracks at the back of Maelog Place, and when she concentrated her hearing she could make out the constant thrum of car engines carrying people in and out of the city. The sounds soothed her. It wasn't the still of the night yet. It wasn't *monster* time. And if she could just get to sleep before then, she'd be all right. Earlier on, she'd heard a choir singing over at the

Church of St Emmanuel and, when the train had finished its breathless journey past, she realised they'd started again. The sound was only faint, but Kate could pick up the strains of the men and women's voices as they surged louder towards the peak of the tune. She didn't know what the song was, but it was pretty. Even cocooned in her nightly battle with the dark, she smiled a little.

But then, almost imperceptibly, something shifted in the night air. A few streets away, a dog set up an anguished howl, joined by two or three more before they whimpered into subdued silence. Kate frowned. Cats shrieked and hissed in the street outside. The music from the church a few hundred metres away faded in her head, the sound draining to nothing and taking the throbbing car engines and the raindrops with it.

Thump. Something landed heavily on the roof and Kate's terrified eyes rolled upwards, her mouth falling open a little. It was too heavy to be a bird or a cat. What was it? Sweat seeped from the palms of her hands into Lucky's fur. *Mummy. She wanted Mummy.* The thing on the roof moved and Kate froze.

With each leaden step taken on top of the house, sound faded from Kate's world. Cold silence oozed through the tiles and down through the attic, its fingers reaching for the little girl, wrapping round her mind and digging sharp nails in, squeezing tighter than she held the tatty toy. Her throat worked to make a scream, but she couldn't find it. For a horrible moment, she couldn't remember how.

The clock beside her bed ceased its quiet, steady electric

tick, even though the luminous hands continued on their regimented journey. Her heart stopped its panicked beat in her ears. Even the inner whine that accompanied complete stillness vanished. Her head was empty, cut off even from the regulation clicks and whirrs of its own body. Alone. Vacant.

The monsters had found her in the dark and they were never ever going to let her go.

And then she gasped and sat bolt upright, air pounding noisily through her lungs, the clock bursting back into life, the rustle of the sheets and duvet an explosion of joyous sound as whatever had been on the roof took a final leap clear of the house.

Kate didn't go to the window. She couldn't bring herself to move, not even when she heard glass shattering just before the choir fell silent. Not even when a shriek of human agony filled the street and her head. She wasn't a big girl. She wanted her night light.

She finally found her own scream fifteen minutes later when the sirens' wails filled the quiet roads outside, but this time no maternal reassurance would calm her. Kate Healey slept in with her parents that night, curled up tight against her mother Cara's back. She stayed there for the rest of the week, and no amount of shouting from Daddy could move her.

Kate Healey had found a fear that made the dark seem like child's play. And it came shrouded in silence.

ONE

Gwen Cooper pulled up outside the Church of St Emmanuel and stepped out of the black SUV before quickly zipping up her fitted leather jacket, flinching a little against the rain. Bloody weather. It had been raining for days and showed no sign of letting up, the sky hanging constantly heavy and grey over the city.

Jack Harkness slammed his door and looked over at her as she tucked her chin into the fitted collar.

'It's only water, Gwen. Pure, natural, recycled for millions of years, good old Earth water.' He grinned. 'This little downpour's probably been through you a few times already. Embrace it!'

She stared at him for a moment.

'Thanks for that insight, Jack. It makes me feel so much warmer and drier.'

'You need a proper jacket.' He looked down at his grey wartime thick wool overcoat, which stopped somewhere around his shins.

Gwen raised an eyebrow. 'You wouldn't catch me dead in something like that.'

'Me neither. But then, what's the chance of that?'

Unable to hold back the smile, Gwen shook her head. 'Actually we have caught you bloody dead in it. You just don't stay that way long.' There was something about Jack that could always make her feel good, even after everything that had happened. She blew her damp fringe out of her face. 'Come on. Let's see what's causing all this excitement.'

The rain forgotten for a moment, Gwen took in the activity around them. Since joining Torchwood, her days in the force sometimes seemed like a distant memory, but she still approached situations like a copper. And there seemed to be a lot of police outside the quiet suburban church for what was reportedly only one dead body. The SUV had slid into a space between two police cars, both of which still had their lights flashing and, amidst the men in plastic suits that scurried to and from the SOCO van, three uniformed constables were stretching a crime-scene cordon around the front of the building.

Side by side, Jack and Gwen took the stairs up to the arched doorway two at a time, their easy confidence enough to deter anyone that might try to stop them. Gwen didn't spot the man between them and the entrance, but Jack did.

'We're Torchwood. We'll be taking over from here.'

'Torchwood?' Concealed in the shadows of the doorway, only the glowing end of his cigarette visible, the man's accent had the gravelly edge of North London.

'Gwen Cooper and Captain Jack Harkness.' Gwen spoke firmly, but the man's dark outline didn't move from blocking the entrance. She glared. 'Let us through please, this is our business now.'

'Well, well, well.' The man laughed drily and stepped out of the gloom. 'I thought you lot had gone down at Canary Wharf.' He threw his half-smoked cigarette down and crushed it with a scuffed lace-up shoe. 'But I guess I've never been that lucky.' He looked up. 'DI Tom Cutler. Murder squad.' He sniffed. 'I'm on secondment from Hammersmith.'

Gwen looked the man up and down. His suit was scruffy and it was obvious he hadn't shaved for a day or two. His eyes were sunk deep into their sockets as if they'd tried to bury themselves somewhere where they wouldn't have to look at the world. She'd seen that look before. Drinker?

'What did you do wrong to make them send you down here?'

The man's eyes hardened, but the sharp grin stayed sliced on his face under his dishevelled blond fringe. 'That's none of your business, even if you are Torchwood.' He leaned forward a little. 'And tell me if I'm getting it wrong, but you lot don't seem too popular among the ordinary rank and file.' He nodded towards the men and women working in the wet road, many of whom cast a suspicious glance over at the two dark-haired plain-clothed strangers.

'All part of the job. Most of them know we're all on the same team at the end of the day.' Jack smiled, but Gwen could see that he was eager to get inside and see the crime scene. The clock was ticking. Still, she was curious and the question tumbled out of her impulsive mouth before she could stop it.

'What do you know about Torchwood anyway?'

'Ran into some nasty trouble in Hammersmith with a case back in 2003. Torchwood came in and dealt with it.' Pulling the collar of his suit jacket up and tugging it round his neck, DI Cutler stepped out into the rain, leaving the doorway clear. 'And back then I was very happy to let them. There were some things that I didn't want as my responsibility.' The smile fell, and for the first time Gwen could see the haunted depth in the man's hollow eyes. Maybe he did drink, but maybe he had good reason to.

'Like whatever happened to that poor sod in there. So be my guest and take the case. It's all yours.' Cutler turned his back on them and headed down the stairs. 'The ME's still inside waiting for you. If you don't want the body, then he'll take it,' he called back over his shoulder. 'And good luck.'

Gwen stared after him. 'Are there a lot of people in the system that know so much about us?'

'Sometimes people are valuable out in the real world with a little knowledge.' Jack watched the disappearing figure with renewed interest. 'I guess Torchwood One figured he'd be a useful ally in the police. And it wasn't like they had Retcon available.' He grinned at Gwen. 'They had to go with good old-fashioned trust. Fancy that.'

She raised a dark eyebrow. 'Trust? It'd never work.'

Jack frowned. 'Well, I bet they had more permanent solutions for when they weren't feeling the love. Maybe our DI Cutler was luckier than he thought.'

Gwen's expression darkened as she took one last look at the shabby figure embracing the gloom. 'Still, it looks like whatever happened to him left him pretty messed up.'

'He'll be fine. Eventually.' Jack turned back to the church. 'Let's get in out of this goddamned rain.'

'It's only water, Jack.' Gwen found her own smile again. 'Good old pure, Earth water. Embrace it.'

Four minutes later, the grin had fallen from Gwen's face. The bright church was empty apart from the plastic-suited medical examiner and a constable at the door, who was very intently facing the thick wood rather than looking in towards the crime scene. Gwen didn't blame him. For a long moment neither she nor Jack spoke, the sound of the rain hammering on the roof keeping time with the thud of her heart and the churn in her stomach. There was a lot of blood.

'I can see why DI Cutler was so keen to hand it over.' Her mouth couldn't decide if it wanted to be wet or dry, and her legs trembled slightly. The body in the church was very definitely dead and, despite all the things she'd seen since joining Torchwood, Gwen was pretty sure she was in a fifty-fifty situation with regards to throwing up. She pushed her hair away from her hot face and took a deep breath. She was buggered if she was going to lose control in front of the police ME. They'd love that back at the station.

Jack crouched beside the body, his eyes running over it thoughtfully. He didn't look up. 'It's OK, doctor. We'll take it from here.'

The ME pulled his plastic hood back and mask down to reveal a pale, middle-aged face. 'Are you sure?'

Jack peered at him through his dark fringe. 'Unless of course you can tell me how this happened?'

The ME shook his head. 'Sorry. Never seen anything like it. It doesn't make sense.' He paused. 'If you figure it out, could you let me know?'

'No can do.'

'Thought not. Bloody Torchwood.' He turned to leave, and for a moment Gwen remembered what it had been like policing when she thought all there was to worry about were human dangers. She found that hard to comprehend, with everything she knew now. God, she hoped Jack never had to Retcon her again. Even if it took all the pain and anger she sometimes felt because of Torchwood, it would also be like turning all the lights out on the world.

'Just one thing.' Jack stood up. 'Was he alone here?'

The ME shook his head. 'No, he was rehearsing with five others. Some classical singing group. One was in the toilet when it happened; the other four have been taken to hospital.'

'Injured?' Gwen asked.

'No, but completely traumatised. None of them would speak. They were just sitting on the front pew huddled together. If that bloke that was in the loo hadn't called the police, they'd probably all still be sitting there now.'

'Thanks.' Jack looked over at Gwen and she nodded. She didn't need telling to make sure they had the names of the witnesses by the time they left. There was a moment of awkward silence.

'Right. I'll leave you to it, then.' The ME sighed. 'I presume you don't want him in here either?' He glanced at the constable down by the church door.

Jack smiled warmly at the man. 'Thanks. We'll let them know outside when we're done. We're going to want to take the body back with us. Oh, and one more thing.' He pulled a small notebook and pen out from somewhere deep in his overcoat and scribbled a number on it. 'Give that to DI Cutler. Tell him I want to know if he sees anything else like this.'

'Will do.' The plastic slippers the ME wore over his shoes whispered as he made his way down to where the constable was waiting, and it was only when the soft thud of the church door shutting echoed through the high archways around them that Jack stood up, his hand on his hips.

'So, what do you think?'

Gwen took a deep breath and looked again at the body that lay spread-eagled in a large pool of congealing blood. She tried not to really see the piece of sheet music that had turned crimson, dropped during the attack and soaked in warm red, the notes all blurring into each other; the music gone for ever from the paper. She tried not to look into the open eyes, whose expression was a photograph of the dead man's last feelings: empty horror, fear and that awful disbelief that something so terrible didn't always happen to other people.

Looking at those things would make her throw up. Those things would muddy her thinking with her feelings, and there wasn't any time for that now. Jack needed more from her. Especially now the team was so much smaller than it had been and had too many of its own empty spaces. She bit the inside of her cheek, enjoying the sharp moment of pain that forced her to focus on the necessity of her job. Taking care to avoid the blood, she moved around the body, assessing it.

The man was in his mid-forties, balding and, judging from the chubbiness in his pale cheeks, probably a little on the overweight side of healthy, but it was hard to truly gauge his mid-section. Something had sliced him open from his chin to his pelvis in what looked like one neat incision. His clothes, skin and the membrane casing beneath were peeled back and lay under his prostrate arms as if he'd unbuttoned a shirt and spread it wide on the floor around him. His freed guts spilled slightly over the edge of his pelvis, a slick grey trail of rotten sausage, but, from what she could make out, the rest of his organs seemed in place. Not that she was an expert on the inner workings of the human body.

'It doesn't look much like a Weevil attack to me,' she said finally.

Jack nodded. 'You're right. A Weevil didn't do this. Weevils are aggressive. Everything about their attacks is uncontrolled and violent. This...' He crouched by the dead man's head. 'This is *precise*. I want to examine the cut when we get back to the Hub. I'm betting he was opened up with one movement. Amazing.' He looked up at Gwen. 'Notice anything missing?'

'What, apart from his skin and any sign of life?' She snorted.

Jack raised an eyebrow. 'Serious moment, Gwen. Look at the body.'

She stared into the red mess. 'I'm not a bloody doctor, Jack. How am I supposed to know?' *I'm not Owen*, that's what she'd really wanted to say, but that would do no one any good. And it was there, unspoken, anyway. She could see it in a moment's clouding in Captain Jack's dark eyes.

'Well, you'd better spend some time studying that wall chart of the human body that's hanging in the Autopsy Room.' His voice was soft, and his own hurt vibrated loudly in it. Her grief was his grief too. Sometimes, she hated herself for getting far too caught up in the ups and downs of being Gwen Cooper to remember that.

She smiled gently, crouching beside him. 'I'll take

21

that as an order.' She peered into the mutilated body. 'So what's missing then?'

Jack pointed at the man's throat just under where it had been cut. 'The voice box and vocal cords.'

Gwen stared. On reflection, the man's neck area did look empty around the spinal column, but she couldn't see any real indication of trauma. 'Were they ripped out?'

Jack shook his head. 'His Adam's apple is fine and the larynx and folds *should* be under it. But it looks more like they were never there. Which would make singing pretty impossible.' He frowned. 'I can't think of any human instrument that could remove something so precisely.'

He touched the almost invisible Bluetooth device in his ear. 'Ianto. You there?'

He paused, and Gwen thought of Ianto Jones sitting in the warmth of the Hub, probably drinking coffee. What he was going to make of this body, she'd be curious to find out. Pizza probably wouldn't be on the menu for dinner.

'Has there been any Rift activity in the area of Gadalfa Street tonight? We're at the Church of St Emmanuel.' Still focused on the call, Jack stood up and Gwen followed. Jack nodded, the reaction to whatever was said in his ear automatic. 'OK. We'll be back at the Hub in about thirty minutes. We're bringing the body with us, so get the Autopsy Room set up.'

The conversation with Ianto over, Jack turned back to Gwen. 'Whatever did this definitely came through the

Rift. There was a spike about an hour ago. Ianto said it started rising a couple of streets away and then peaked here. Here and gone within minutes.'

Smiling, Gwen rested a hand playfully on one tilted hip of her jeans. 'I could have told you that when we first got here. Without any of your missing vocal cords and Rift spikes.'

'Oh really?' Jack's eyes danced. 'Then share, PC Cooper.'

Looking upwards, Gwen pointed at the once-impressive stained-glass window high against the wall. It had shattered inwards, coloured shards decorating the area hidden in shadows along a far wall.

'No human criminal would come through a window that high when they could just use the bloody door.' Grinning slightly, she raised an eyebrow and swung her hips as she strode past Jack up the aisle and towards the exit. 'I'll tell the uniforms they can come and clean up now, shall I?'

Jack was staring up at the window, smiling. 'I guess the pizza's on me for that then, huh?'

Gwen laughed, and headed out into the rain.

TWO

The lift purred quietly as it lowered Ianto Jones down into the hidden heart of the Hub.

His suit jacket was damp from the rain that had been falling all evening, but he didn't mind. He'd needed a quick natural freshen up to help give himself some extra energy and, although the doughnuts that were still warm in the bag he was carrying probably weren't the best brain food, they'd certainly go well with the fresh pot of coffee he'd left brewing.

His shoulders ached slightly from sitting peering at the various computer screens for far too long and, for a few moments after he'd stood up, his tired eyes had had difficulty focusing. No wonder Tosh had worn glasses. Ianto was finding that as the days wore on without her, his admiration for his dead colleague's abilities was growing. And it wasn't as if he'd lacked respect for her while she was alive.

His face tingled pleasantly from the rain, but it was going to take more than a five-minute walk outdoors to relax him. It seemed like he'd been trying to figure out the intricacies of Tosh's various computer programs for ever and, while he was no IT dunce, Toshiko had been in a different league. Even with her little pop-up help icons, a lot of what she'd set up was way beyond him.

The heavy metal door slid open and he stepped into the warm light of the Hub, ignoring the computer stations and heading towards the Autopsy Room. The pop-ups had made him smile though, even if each one had sent a needle of grief into his heart. Typical of Toshiko to have planned for every eventuality.

'And once again Cardiff is alive with the sound of music as the city prepares for the fifth annual Welsh Amateur Operatic Contest…' The TV screen quietly delivered the news and, putting the doughnuts down, Ianto looked for the remote. He sometimes liked background noise while he was working, tonight being one of those nights, but Jack definitely didn't. 'The best singers from across the nation have arrived in preparation for the finals which will be held in front of a star-studded judging panel eleven days from now, in a live television broadcast from the Millennium Centre…'

Ianto clicked her off and followed the crisp scent of fresh coffee to the bubbling machine. Coffees in hand, he took the steps down into the Autopsy Room. He froze as he saw the body.

'Jesus.'

Jack looked up. 'Not even close. This is Richard Greenwood, 45, from Newport.'

'What happened to him?' Ianto had completely forgotten about the coffees, but dimly noticed Gwen taking them from him. 'Don't tell me a Weevil.'

'Then I won't.' Jack moved round to the other side of the exposed corpse and carefully lifted one flap of peeled-back skin. 'And it wasn't. Whatever did this was something else.' He frowned. 'He was opened up in one movement from his throat all the way down, but look, this is fascinating…'

'I think I can see well enough from here.' Staying where he was and watching his two colleagues peering intently at the mutilated man, Ianto wasn't sure whether he should be envious or slightly nervous of Jack and Gwen's ability to cope with gore on this level. He knew his own limitations.

'I see it!' Gwen exclaimed. 'The skin and his clothes.' She looked up. 'It's like they've been melted together.'

Jack nodded. 'More like fused. Weird, huh?'

Gwen came round to the other side of the examining table and lifted the man's skin, his blue, bloodstained shirt rising with it. 'See?'

Ianto gritted his teeth and nodded. 'That's… great.'

Jack raised an eyebrow. 'Brings a whole new meaning to a fitted shirt.'

Leaning back against the wall, Ianto reached for his drink. The coffee didn't seem as appealing as it had ten minutes ago, but the scalding taste of it was just what his system needed to fight the vague sense of nausea that drifted through his gut. The doughnuts were a definite pass though.

'Any reason for the attack?' Deliberately ignoring the body, Ianto looked across at Jack.

'Not as far as we know. We'll need to run some deeper checks on the victim, but he worked in a bank, paid his mortgage on time, a wife, but no kids. Pretty much an ordinary Joe.'

'Except that now he's dead.'

'Yes, and whatever killed him took his vocal cords and larynx as a souvenir.'

His nausea overwhelmed by his curiosity, Ianto looked into the exposed neck of the victim. 'Why on Earth would someone do that?' He paused. 'And how?'

Jack shrugged. 'I guess that's what we need to find out.' He reached for his own coffee. 'So tell me about the Rift.'

'Well, there seems to have been an increase in activity since that electrical storm four nights ago, but mainly low-level stuff. I've been running some more analysis on that data and from what I can tell…' Ianto looked from Jack's expectant gaze to Gwen's and back again. 'Well, remembering that I'm not an expert, I think maybe that storm wasn't an entirely natural phenomenon.'

'What do you mean?'

'I think there *was* a storm over Cardiff, but I think the electrical part of it came in from the Rift, and the two mixed as they met. Maybe that storm was also the arrival of something alien.'

Jack frowned over at Gwen. 'Didn't we check the storm's readings at the time?'

'Don't look at me.' Gwen shook her dark hair. 'I was at home tucked up in bed with Rhys and we were whipping up our own electrical storm, thank you.'

Jack turned his attention to him, and Ianto felt his face burn as he stumbled over his words. 'We were here, but we were… busy.'

Jack suddenly grinned. 'Oh yeah, so we were.'

From the corner of his eye, Ianto could see Gwen looking from one man to the other, and he concentrated on sipping his coffee. It wasn't as if she didn't know about him and Jack, but it still felt strange whenever there was any open reference to it.

Gwen giggled, breaking the awkward moment. 'It seems like we all had our eyes off the ball, then.'

Jack flashed his best boyish smile. 'Or on it, depending on your perspective.'

'So, what next?' Listening to the banter, Ianto gave up feeling embarrassed.

'Let's get the body on ice for the night, and then see if you can find any connections between the Rift activity from the storm and the spike from tonight. At least then we'll know we're dealing with a recent arrival.' Jack looked over to Gwen. 'You might as well go home. We can go to the hospital and talk to the witnesses in the morning.'

'Are you sure?'

'Sure I'm sure.' He winked. 'Now get out of here.'

Ianto picked up his coffee. 'Right, I'll get on with that analysis.'

'Not so fast, big boy.' Jack nodded towards the body. 'You can take the feet end. We need to get him on a trolley.'

Groaning, Ianto reached for the shoes, and hoped he wasn't grimacing. There were some things he was never going to get used to about working at Torchwood.

THREE

The windscreen wipers on the old Ford Escort squealed gently as they battered the rain from side to side with the regular beat of a metronome. Peering out into the night, Dyllis Llewelyn clutched the handbag on her knee a little tighter. There weren't even lights on this section of the road, and there hadn't been for the past few miles. She let a small sigh out into the slowly building tense atmosphere. It felt like they'd been on this journey for an eternity.

If they'd left the farm at three like she'd suggested, they'd have been in Cardiff by now but, as it was, Barry had to make sure everyone had their instructions four times over before picking up the car keys, and it had been gone seven when they'd finally driven out of the gates. As if their boys didn't know the farm like the backs of their hands. They'd been working it since they could walk; both she and Barry had insisted on that. Theirs was a family farm, and it was going to stay that way.

Her brow furrowed, trying in vain to make out any shapes in the darkness, but all she could see were drops of rain smearing down her passenger window. She glanced at the dials on the dashboard. The clock glowed 11.15, and she stifled a yawn. Barry would no doubt blame her for their late arrival at the B & B, but she'd had to stop for dinner, even if the Happy Cook was 'an overpriced rip-off'. Since her illness she had too many pills to take, and if she took them without food they would make her sick. Still, it wasn't Barry's fault that she probably hadn't explained that to him. They didn't have the kind of marriage where you talked about things. You just got on with it and made do.

Next to her, his eyes firmly on the white line in the road whose dashes added silent harmony to the windscreen wipers, Barry hummed through his octaves, up and down, over and over. Even just doing something as simple as those exercises, anyone could hear that he had a beautiful voice. It was a true Welshman's voice, full of the natural power of the solid land and valleys that had bred it, hundreds of years of history and courage carried in every tune. There was nothing namby-pamby about the way Barry Llewelyn sang, not like those pancaked West End performers from London. When her Barry sang, people noticed.

Still, as she watched the slightly smug tilt to her

husband's chin, for the first time his singing voice seemed a little sour to her. She couldn't help but think he was happy they weren't singing as a couple this time around, and that made her sad. It was singing in the church that had brought them together all those years ago; she the best soprano and he the best tenor, and neither of them had been a bad looker along with it.

She thought of how her own hair was greying and, looking at the creases and crags that covered her husband's face, she wondered what had happened to those two young people who loved to make music together. In fact, they'd loved doing a lot of things together back then, but twenty-odd years of marriage and hard farm life could knock that out of the best of couples.

Ahead, the lights of Cardiff appeared glowing in a distant pool of light that only served to make the darkness around the car even more suffocating. Or maybe it was the atmosphere *inside* the car that was strangling her. Looking at the knots and veins that had appeared on the backs of her hands over the past few months, she wondered if Barry ever thought of her affectionately any more. She'd always believed that even though they never really talked or laughed together in the way she saw people do on the telly, they'd had a quiet foundation of love underneath it all.

When the national singing competition had begun, a light had come back on in Barry's eyes and they'd started smiling at each other again. And they hadn't done badly, coming second and third in their category in two of the four years it had been running. She'd known she was the weaker singer, but she hadn't thought it really mattered.

Not until she had the stroke at any rate. Her dry fingers rose and touched the slight dip at the left edge of her mouth. No more singing for her. Apart from losing some of her ability to shape the sounds, her bloody brain couldn't guarantee her all the words to a song any more. It made her feel like a helpless, ugly fool. Not that they'd talked about *that* either. They'd just got on with it and made do. But she was sure she'd seen the glint in her husband's eyes when the doctors had told her she wouldn't be taking part in this year's competition, and it was a look that broke her heart. He badly wanted to win, and she'd never realised. Was his life lacking so much?

It seemed clear to Dyllis that Barry was almost glad that she'd had her stroke. And they didn't talk about *that* either. Although these days she sometimes couldn't find the right words for things anyway, like that time she'd gone to the post office and kept insisting poor Enid at the counter give her a pound of bananas rather than the six first-glass, *class not glass*, stamps she'd wanted. Maybe that side effect was a blessing. It seemed to Dyllis, as the road carried them into the outskirts of Cardiff, that the only way for a marriage to survive was *not* to communicate. If you started talking, just where would you stop?

'Shit!' The octaves forgotten for a moment, Barry's voice was full of the earth of the farm as he wrestled with the steering wheel while the car suddenly shuddered, jolting them across the road. The Escort cut across the white lines, slewing into the opposite carriageway, and Barry finally braked, bringing them to a halt up against the barrier at the other side of the road.

For a moment they sat, just wrapped in their breathing, Dyllis slowly releasing her death grip on her handbag, and Barry leaning into the wheel.

'Bloody blowout.' His head turned slowly in her direction and his eyes were soft and full of dread as he reached over and squeezed her knee. 'You OK, love?'

Dyllis nodded and smiled. Her thin shoulder hurt where the seatbelt had dug in and her heart was pounding hard in her chest, but the warmth and care in her husband's touch almost made the accident worthwhile. Maybe she'd been hard on him. Maybe her stroke had made her brain play tricks on her. Maybe there was some love left, after all.

'Are you sure?' Barry stared intently at her head, as if he thought the shock might bring on another stroke, *the* stroke, the one that would leave her with more to worry about than stamps and bananas.

'Really, I'm fine.' She squeezed his hand.

'Right. You stay here while I change the tyre. We'll be at that B & B in no time.' His eyes drifted away and his smile was awkward on his face. Watching him get out of the car, Dyllis knew that he was sorry. Sorry that they'd left so late, sorry about her stroke, and sorry that he was excited to sing on his own. It was funny the things you could say in a marriage without really saying anything at all.

'I'll come too.' Leaving her best handbag in the footwell, she stepped outside.

Although they were right on the edge of the city, the road was dark, only the beam from the torch Barry was working with casting long shadows across the tarmac. The rain had eased to a light mist dusting her cheeks, and the breeze that carried it whispered a chill at her neck. Shivering, Dyllis pulled her coat tight round her.

'Are you all right?' she asked.

'Yes, just need to change the tyre.' Barry's disembodied voice drifted from the other side. The jack clunked on the hard ground, and Dyllis could hear her husband's concentrated breath as he worked the machine and the car slowly rose. Somewhere in the distance an owl hooted, and the lost trees rustled on either side of the road, their shapes simple darker outlines against the midnight blue of the sky. It was like the depths of the ocean, she thought, twisting to look at the trees behind her. Anything could be in there, but you just couldn't see it.

Beyond the low metal crash railing was a line of thick, gnarled trunks, rising up into shadowy branches that creaked and entwined themselves to create a barrier of nature. A border not to be crossed. Dyllis looked back at the broken car and the thick tarmac of the road, and then the crash barrier on the other side. They were trapped in the road. She shivered again, this time trying to shake her feeling of unease. This was ridiculous. She wasn't a child. There was nothing to be afraid of in the dark.

Barry emerged from beside the car, and pulled the

spare tyre out of the well in the boot, replacing it with the damaged wheel. He grinned at her. 'If you want to warm up, you could collect up the bits of rubber we've left all over the road and dump them on the side. Probably dangerous to leave them out here.'

Dyllis nodded, staring out across the road around her. Maybe she should have stayed in the car. Wandering around in that gloom didn't seem too appealing. She swallowed hard, and then realised Barry was looking at her, mildly amused.

'Don't you tell me you're scared of the dark after all these years, Dyllis Llewelyn. You and me have crossed pitch-black fields to get to stuck sheep and cows in early labour. What's the matter with you, woman?'

He was teasing, not scolding her, and she laughed a little and shrugged. 'Must just be city nights that scare me.'

'Tell you what...' He heaved the wheel into position. 'Why don't we have a song?'

'Oh, don't be so daft.'

'You never used to think it was daft to sing with me.' He screwed in the first wheel nut. 'Come on, it's only you and me. If you forget the words, just hum it.'

Dyllis looked at a piece of torn rubber lying damaged in the middle of the road. She should really go and get it. 'Well, what shall we sing?' She took three furtive steps away from the car.

'La Traviata. Un Di Felice.' Barry's voice floated out to her. 'It's our best one.'

She smiled. They'd come second with that the year before last. The judges said they'd never heard it sung so beautifully by untrained singers.

They didn't pause to count in. Barry and Dyllis Llewelyn just started singing into the night. Her lungs opening, and letting the words flow without any conscious thought, Dyllis started to relax. She picked up the first piece of heavy torn rubber and tossed it towards the side of the road. Something rustled in the undergrowth, the noise climbing high into the tree.

Dyllis stared, the music in her throat faltering. Behind her, even though he was in a crouched position, Barry's voice soared: a lyrical bird in flight, set free to reach the skies. It was beautiful. Even in her best days, she hadn't come close to that quality of sound. Dyllis could sing a tune, but when Barry sang it was as if he poured all those things they didn't talk about into the melody.

The rustling moved to another tree, as if some watching creature had jumped from one to another. Taking two steps back, Dyllis looked up, the song frozen in her now. Barry didn't seem to notice her quietness, his half of the duet still filling the silent night as he fixed the spare tyre in place.

There was something in the tree. Something bad. Cold crept up through Dyllis's toes and fingers, and she started to tremble. Her eyes wide, she peered into the gloom of the overhanging canopy. In the middle of the twisted, shadowy shapes was an area of complete darkness. A blackness that was beyond empty. Her mouth falling open, she tried to breathe but, looking into that awful nothingness, it seemed that everything she knew was being drained from inside. Behind her, Barry's singing faded, the sound sucked away, pulled back from her ears.

Barry. Her brain kept that word, focusing on it. *Barry, not bananas, not six first-glass bananas, but Barry.* She stumbled back to the car.

As if from outside herself, she saw her husband's smile fall as he slammed the boot, wiping his hands on his trousers. His lips were moving but she couldn't hear his words. Her heart wanted to explode from silent emptiness. Feeling her lips moving and knowing she was screaming something, but only hoping from within the deathly quiet in her mind that she was finding the right words, she pushed her husband to the front of the car, before scrabbling round to get in herself.

It was only when she had the door shut and had desperately pushed down the locks that she could finally hear herself rasping 'Drive… Drive… Drive…' over and over. Peering back between the seats, she was sure she saw the dark space move into the road and start to re-form itself into some kind of shape just as Barry pulled away, tugging the car back onto the right side of the road, and speeding towards the city.

For five long minutes neither of them spoke, Barry staring intently at the road, and Dyllis gripping the back of the seat as she stared out of the rear-view mirror. Then, as they approached the bright lights of Cardiff, she heard her heart beating normally inside her chest, and that awful sense of emptiness slid away from her. She leaned back in her seat and sighed. Every sound seemed fresh and clear and beautiful.

Barry looked over at her. 'Jesus, Dyllis. What the hell was that about?'

She stared through the windscreen. He wasn't going to believe her. She could hear it in the harshness of his voice. 'There was something…' What had there been? How could she explain it? 'There was something in the trees. Something bad.'

She didn't look at her husband. She knew what she'd see. A man biting his lip when he really wanted to yell, and a man who was scared that maybe there was something going wrong in his wife's head other than the effects of the stroke. Either way, by the time they finally pulled up at the small bed and breakfast, not too far from the Bay, the happy moment they'd shared was truly gone. They slept in silence.

FOUR

Even though the day outside was grey and overcast, the bright lights of the hospital dispersed any hint of the rain with no-nonsense professionalism. Peering through the small glass window of the door separating the corridor from the recreation room, Gwen studied the four witnesses. Where the rest of the chairs were in semi-circular rows aimed at the focal point of the television, or on either side of two small tables by the collection of board games, the singers had pulled theirs into a short line as close together as possible, so that the scratched and worn arm of each was touching the next.

Gwen frowned, two neat lines pulling in between her eyebrows and resting for a moment in the space where one day in the future they'd settle for good. Something about the way these people were sat reminded her of being a child and wanting to be as near to your best friend as you could be so you could giggle about boys and pass notes. But none of these four were children; in fact they were far from it.

A woman sat at the end of the row, her head hanging forward, her long blonde hair obscuring her features above the dressing gown that was pulled tightly around her slim figure. She was probably the youngest of the four, perhaps in her late twenties. Gwen thought through the descriptions she'd got from the scene of crime team and ticked the blonde off as Magaly East. Next to Magaly were two men, Paul Davies and John Geoghan, neither particularly striking in any way and both in their forties. Another woman bookended them, steely-haired although probably younger than she looked. She had to be Rhiannon Cave.

Gwen frowned. The TV was on, but none of the four seemed to be watching the daytime chat show on the screen. Two were just staring in silence at an area of wall just beyond it and, whilst their mouths were moving, it didn't look as if they were having a conversation together. Gwen breathed out, fogging the glass. They were strange, but at least they were awake.

Her foot tapped, impatient for Jack to come back with the nurse and the tray of teas. The nurse had described the mental state of all the singers as 'fragile' and said that they had disturbed the other patients on the ward with their rantings when they emerged from their catatonic states in the early hours of the morning. They knew they had been put in the recreation room to be interviewed by the police, and Gwen knew that the longer she waited the more agitated they would become, if they were as delicate as they seemed.

Glancing at her watch, Gwen sighed. Jack had been gone for much longer than it took to work a vending machine, even in an NHS hospital. The corridor yawned endlessly to her right, occupied only by a slim nurse, whose skirt rustled softly as she carefully filled pill boxes from a trolley of jars. She didn't look up.

Gwen bit her lip. There was no point in just hanging around like some constable waiting for the boss. She might as well get started on her own. The nurse had been quite pretty and it was obvious she'd fancied Jack and, as much as it wasn't like him to seriously flirt on the job, he may well have got distracted. She grinned slightly. Bloody Jack and his sex appeal. If only they could find some alien technology that could extract that, they could all retire early.

Leaving the pale green of the corridor behind, she pushed the door open and immediately the lines between her eyes re-formed. Phillip Schofield's pat laugh filled her head, and she glared at the machine in the corner. God, that television was turned up loud, not that the four witnesses seemed bothered by it.

Pulling a chair towards them, she smiled gently. 'Hi.' She spoke softly. 'I'm Gwen Cooper. I'd like to ask you some questions about last night if that's OK.'

The blonde woman on the end rocked steadily

backwards and forwards, but lifted her head slightly so that her bloodshot tired eyes were fixed intently on Gwen.

This time both Schofield and his guest laughed together behind her, cutting a path between Gwen and the people opposite. 'Would it be all right if I turned that television off? It's very loud.'

As one, all four witnesses vigorously shook their heads. The older woman on the end, Rhiannon Cave, leaned forward. 'We want to hear it. We want the sound.' She spat the words out in an urgent hiss, and Gwen recoiled slightly. There was a dark defensiveness in the woman's eyes that hinted at the edge of madness. Her mouth twitched as she sat back in her chair, her jaw moving as she ground her teeth and stared defiantly at Gwen.

For a moment Gwen said nothing, reassessing the situation. They were obviously more disturbed by what they'd seen than she'd expected. Maybe she should have waited for Jack. She could see why the nurse had called them fragile. As far as Gwen could tell, they were beyond fragile. They were nearer broken.

Four sets of eyes stared at her and each of the witnesses held the hand of the person next to them so tightly that the whites of their knuckles seemed to be in danger of ripping through the skin. It was as if they were terrified someone was suddenly going to try to pull them apart. Watching them, Gwen had a moment of clarity. The aggression she'd seen in Rhiannon Cave's eyes was actually hiding an awful, deep-seated fear. Why else would they be clinging to each other like that?

Despite a vague sense of revulsion she couldn't understand, Gwen leaned forward a little. 'I know that this is very upsetting for you, but we need to try and understand what happened to Richard Greenwood.' Magaly East rocked a little harder, and Gwen wondered if her nails had pierced the soft palm of the man next to her. If they had, he didn't seem to notice.

'I just need you to tell me what you can remember about what happened in the church last night while you were rehearsing.'

None of the four spoke, but Gwen could feel their tension and anguish intensifying. It came off them in waves. She pushed on, lowering her own voice in an attempt to subconsciously calm them.

'If you could just give me some idea of what the man that did this to your friend looked liked, then it will help us catch him.'

Magaly East twitched and with her free hand tugged her thin white dressing gown around her a little tighter. Her eyes drifted to somewhere beyond Gwen.

'It came through the window.' Her voice sounded like smashed glass, as if it had encapsulated the memory. 'It was… it was…' Her mouth twitched and then she sobbed, curling over herself so that her head was almost resting on her knees as she cried.

Gwen looked at the other three, their faces distraught, expressions pulling their skin this way and that as they fought images in their minds. Despite wanting to leave them in peace, Gwen pressed on. She needed to know. Torchwood needed to know.

'It was what?'

The man next to the sobbing Magaly shook his head and frowned. 'I can't remember. I can't remember. I can't remember.'

Rhiannon Cave moaned, her mouth drifting open. 'There was this shape… this black shape.' She hesitated. 'More than black. It was awful. And then I felt… I felt…'

'I can't remember. I can't remember. I can't remember.' The man barked the sentences out, and Gwen flinched trying to hear past him to what Rhiannon Cave was trying to say. Magaly East's sobbing grew louder and the anguish in it carved into Gwen's heart. What had happened to these people? What was it they'd seen that could have this effect on them?'

'You felt what, Ms Cave?'

The man who hadn't spoken shook his head slightly. 'Desolate.'

Magaly Betts leaned over so that her head rested on the knee of the man beside her, all four huddling in tighter.

'It was silent.' The man frowned.

'As if there was no one else there. Ever.' Rhiannon Cave's free hand flew to her mouth and her eyes widened. 'I want it out of my head.' She grabbed at Gwen. 'I want to forget. Please make it go away.'

Pushing her chair away, Gwen stood up, trying to gently but firmly extricate herself from the clutching hands. 'I'm sorry, I—' Her foot almost tripped backwards over a coffee table as she stumbled away. The noise in the room was rising, the crying and shouting merging into one.

'I don't remember, I don't remember, I don't remember, I don't remember...'

'Make it go away! Please!'

'So alone. Such silence...'

Needing to get out, to find some sanity, Gwen abandoned any hope of trying to calm them herself. They needed sedatives. They needed bloody Retcon. What the hell were they dealing with here?

Pushing out through the door, she collided with Jack and the nurse coming in.

The nurse's face fell. 'What have you done, you stupid woman?' She didn't wait for an answer before scurrying into the recreation room, pressing the bell for assistance as she did so.

'I'm really sorry, Jack. I just asked them some questions and...'

Jack grabbed her arm, tugging her down the corridor. 'You can tell me on the way.'

'On the way to where?'

'Cutler rang. He says another body's been found.'

Happy to leave that terrible anguish behind, Gwen broke into a slight jog to keep up with Jack. She'd be back though, she promised herself. As soon as she could. And she'd bring some Retcon with her.

FIVE

On the other side of town, Adrienne Scott pulled her BMW into the small car park at the back of the Havannah Court Autism Centre and sat for a second after turning the engine off. She stared at the familiar bricks of the wall in front of her. It seemed she knew every uneven edge of them, but then she'd used this space a lot over the past four years. This was *her* space. On a Monday, Wednesday and Friday at any rate. Maybe using the same slot on each visit was her homage to autism, her own little need for regularity.

Her dark bob sank back into the headrest. She just needed a minute or two of peace before going inside. Ryan was her son and she loved him. She was sure she *must* love him on some level, but it was all just so damned hard when there was nothing but anxiety given in return. She was his mother; she'd grown him inside her and kept him safe, and he couldn't stand her touch. How could that be, she wondered for the millionth time since Ryan's diagnosis, even though she knew the question was pointless.

Not just her touch, she reminded herself. *Any* touch. But she was his mother. It should be different with her. The clock in the dashboard clicked on to ten o'clock, and she reluctantly got out of the car and headed inside, feeling so much older than her thirty-five years.

Signing in, she flashed a tight smile at Sylvia the receptionist, hoping to avoid conversation. No matter what the woman said it always made Adrienne feel guilty. She could hear the innocuous words coming out – '*How's work? Any exciting cases? Isn't it a lovely day? Have you got any plans for the summer? What a smart suit…*' – but it was as if underneath each sentence was the whisper of '*Bad mother. You should have your child at home. Bad mother.*'

Sylvia was still speaking when Adrienne turned her back on her. Adrienne didn't care. Most of the staff at the centre didn't like her, she was pretty sure of that. They thought she was cold; you didn't have to be a mind reader to see that. And maybe she was. Maybe the past six years had made her that way. Some people just weren't cut out to deal with children that were *different*. They had no right to judge her. After all, it was *bad mothers* like her that kept them in their jobs.

A dull ache of tension already creeping into her shoulders, she made her way along the familiar route to

Ryan's room, trying not to look through any of the open doors as she went, but invariably unable to stop herself. This was her penance: one hour, three times a week. She may as well punish herself properly.

She passed 11-year-old Eleanor, whose long hair was always matted no matter how often it was brushed and who would for ever be known as *the dribbling girl* inside Adrienne's head. Turning the corner, she glanced into Michael's room, and sure enough he was still intent on trying to fit a square plastic shape into a round hole simply because the shape and the hole were the same bright red colour. Ryan's nurse, Ceri, had told her that Michael could sit for hours with that block in his hand, trying to squeeze it into the hole. Adrienne wondered if the child would ever see the irony. All these children were square pegs in round holes. How the nurses that worked here didn't end up shaking them out of sheer frustration she would never understand. But then, she was a *bad mother*. She hadn't been able to cope with Ryan for more than eighteen months.

Three doors down from her son's room, a little girl she didn't recognise stared at the wall and screamed as a nurse tried to wipe the snot that streamed down her face. Adrienne turned away in disgust, and the first edge of a headache throbbed loudly at the back of her skull. At least Ryan wasn't a screamer. Staring at the door she had to go through, she ran her manicured fingers through her sleek hair and wished she could raise more enthusiasm for seeing her beautiful son. No, Ryan didn't scream. Ryan was too busy singing. Constantly. All day. From waking to sleeping, barely pausing for breath between songs. Maybe if he'd just been quiet she could have coped. Maybe.

Through the doorway drifted a perfect imitation of Aled Jones's 'Walking In The Air'. Disc 1, track 4. Even she knew their order by heart now. Damn that ex-husband and his *Classical Tracks* CD that he'd played over and over in the car when Ryan was a baby. She hadn't even liked the music then. The too-familiar song slid past her eardrums and wormed its way towards the hammer of pain beating at the back of her skull, adding melody to its rhythm. And damn her baby's autistic memory storing every note and word in its banks until his body was developed enough to endlessly reproduce them.

As Adrienne stepped inside and grimaced a smile at Ceri, Ryan's tune didn't even waver.

SIX

The Bay View Beverley Bed and Breakfast wasn't quite close enough to the bright lights of the Cardiff Bay area to charge premium rates, but being within walking distance it could be guaranteed a steady trade throughout any busy months. Still, Gwen wasn't entirely sure that the owners would be able to fight a false advertising claim if it ever went to court. She reckoned that to consider yourself Bay side, you'd have to at least be able to see the Bay from some part of the building, even if it was only the attic.

The owners in question, Mr and Mrs Beverley, both in their early fifties, were sat sipping tea in their small, overly dressed dining room along with the five or six other guests who had been unfortunate enough to be in the building during that morning's incident. Passing them to head up the stairs, it was clear they were all badly shaken.

Even from a distance, Gwen could see an old-fashioned teacup trembling in one man's hand as a policewoman took a seat opposite him. She could understand that tremble. She still felt a little unsettled after her encounter at the hospital.

'Make sure we get copies of all their notes.' Jack headed up the narrow, steep stairs. 'I doubt they'll have anything solid to give us, but it'll all help.'

Nodding, Gwen looked down at the royal blue carpet. It was threadbare in patches, and, although the skirting boards were clean, they were chipped and tatty and could do with replacing. Maybe the Bay View Beverley Bed and Breakfast wasn't doing so well after all. How was a murder going to affect their business? No wonder the middle-aged couple looked so worried.

The police photographer gave her a brief nod as he squeezed past, heading downstairs, and Gwen thought he looked as pale as his plastic suit. Whatever had happened up there wasn't going to be pretty. But then she wasn't expecting it to be after what they'd seen in the church. At least she, Jack and the police had some idea of what they would find. Whichever of the Beverleys had discovered the body hadn't had that privilege. How long would it be before the B & B would be on the market?

More uniformed officers trotted past them on the narrow stairwell, disgruntled expressions clouding their faces, clearly not happy to be relinquishing another crime scene to the mysterious Torchwood team.

Reaching the top of the building, Gwen followed Jack

round the tight corner and through a door with a tacky ceramic sign with roses and lilac growing around a black number 7. She idly wondered whether someone should point out to the Beverleys that maybe a trip to Ikea wouldn't do their style any harm. Perhaps today wasn't the day for that. Her internal flippancy in the situation surprised her, and she wasn't sure whether she liked it or was appalled by it. Shaking her hair a little, she tried to get a grip on herself and concentrate.

'Well, well.' Detective Inspector Cutler was standing in the middle of the double bedroom, his hands stuffed deep in his trouser pockets, his suit jacket undone. 'It's Mulder and Scully.'

He smiled and, although his eyes were brighter, Gwen thought he looked as scruffy first thing in the morning as he had done late at night. Even though his suit was smart and his shirt tucked in, there was something about him that seemed to her as if he'd just tumbled out of bed. And he still hadn't shaved. Looking at his broad chest and crumpled face, she had to admit there was something attractive about him. In fact, a part of her would have quite liked to see him tumbling out of her bed. Or into it.

As if confirming he was having the same thoughts, Jack gave the policeman a broad grin. 'We must stop meeting like this.'

Cutler raised an eyebrow. 'Trust me, I'd be happy to.' He nodded towards the small en suite bathroom. 'He's in there.' Stepping aside, he made room for Jack and Gwen.

'It's not pretty. His name's Barry Llewelyn, 49, checked in late last night with his wife. He's here for the singing competition. Just like the other one. And, as you can see, he's gone out the same way.'

Gwen moved into the doorway and froze for a moment. Her stomach lurched slightly, acid burning its way up into her chest before, swallowing hard, she controlled it. In many ways, this crime scene was far worse than the one they'd dealt with in the Church of St Emmanuel the previous night, if it was at all possible for the sight of one man cut open from the throat to the pelvis to be preferable to another one.

'How come Ianto gets to stay back at the Hub?' she said softly.

Jack clenched his jaw. 'We have stronger stomachs.'

'I'm glad you're sure about that.'

Unlike the church, the en suite was tiny. As the man had died, his blood had splattered all over the walls, the crimson splashes demanding attention against the purity of the tiles. Handprints blurred down the inside of the cubicle where the victim had obviously tried to stay upright in the face of his terrible attacker. The shower head had come loose from its holder and hung down on its hose, peering over the body with useless concern.

Barry Llewelyn was naked. He might have been a strong man when he was alive, but lying on the lino of the tiny shower room and toilet, his body slightly arched and positioned somewhere half-in, half-out of the shower, his legs looked skinny and insubstantial, too pale from blood loss, their whiteness blending in with the ceramic of the toilet bowl that his foot touched. The muscles of his upper arms had slackened, appearing flabby as they reached outwards to the walls. As with the victim in the church, Barry Llewelyn's torso had been peeled open, his skin an unwrapped towel around his delicate organs.

Gwen fought the urge to grab a sheet from the bedroom and cover him over. There was something vaguely pathetic about the sight of any naked middle-aged man and the fact that this one was terribly mutilated didn't detract from that. She was only glad that his face was turned the other way and she didn't have to look into his dead eyes. It was a sight she'd never really got used to. She wondered for a moment what he'd find to say if they could use a resurrection glove on him. Looking at the way his insides were exposed and throat damaged, she guessed he'd probably be saying bugger all. Despite her own black humour, she shivered. Aside from the fact that it had nearly killed her, there were a million other reasons to be glad that the resurrection glove was one piece of alien technology they wouldn't be using again.

Jack peered into the man's exposed throat.

'Are they missing?' Gwen asked.

Jack stood up. 'Yep.'

'The vocal cords and larynx?' Cutler spoke from behind them. 'I noticed that too.'

Turning away from the body, both Gwen and Jack stared at him. He shrugged.

'It may be your jurisdiction, and to be honest your

57

problem and amen to that, but I'm still curious.' The Detective Inspector sat on the edge of the unmade bed. 'I took a good look at the police photographs last night.' He smiled, and Gwen wondered if it was the wistful quality in that damaged expression that made him so attractive.

'Did they help you sleep?' Jack asked.

'Ha. No.' Cutler frowned. 'But I figured that the killer wouldn't have opened up the poor bastard that precisely for nothing.'

'And you were right,' Jack interrupted. 'I guess you know more about anatomy than Scully here, but we'd be grateful if you could keep your findings to yourself.'

Cutler held up his hands. 'Trust me, I'm not looking to steal Torchwood's glory.' He sighed. 'But if all this gets out…' He ruffled the mess of his hair. 'We all know it *will* get out. And as soon as it does, I'm going to be in the firing line from the press. So the quicker you have some answers, the happier I'll be.'

Jack nodded. 'You and me both. So give me what your guys got before we got here.'

'Not too much to report.' Cutler smiled grimly. 'At 9.15 this morning the vic was in the shower. Singing, according to the couple in the room next door. After about five minutes, they heard glass smashing, which must have been the bathroom window.' He glanced up at Jack. 'And then Llewelyn stopped singing. After a few seconds he started screaming, but that didn't last long. The neighbours heard the wife banging on the bathroom door, and then they went and got the owners.' He paused.

'They called us. I called you.'

Jack looked at the open suitcase on the floor, and the tub of face cream on the small dresser. 'So where's the wife now?'

'The hospital. There's no point trying to speak to her. She's had a massive stroke. Apparently she had a mild one last year. I guess seeing her husband's insides on the outside was enough to bring on the big one.'

Gwen glared at him, in part for his insensitivity, and in part to reprimand herself for finding him quite so sexy when she was so recently married. Still, she thought, looking at the craggy lines that ran down his cheek where dimples might lie if he ever really laughed out loud, there was no harm in looking, was there?

Cutler noticed the look. 'Sorry. Tactlessness is part of my charm.'

Gwen turned back to the crime scene. She frowned. 'The bathroom cabinet mirror's broken. It looks like it's been punched.'

'I thought maybe it was done by Llewelyn fighting back,' Cutler said.

Jack's expression was grim. 'Or maybe whatever did this is getting angrier.'

There was a long pause which Cutler finally broke.

'Oh, that's great. Whatever, not whoever. I thought I'd left all this weird crap behind after everything that happened last time.' He stood up and stared at Jack for a long moment before releasing a sardonic smile. 'Good luck with it.'

He was at the bedroom door when his mobile rang out: no trendy song or humorous sound effect, just the shrill clear tone cutting through the air.

'Cutler.' The handset pressed to his ear he looked up at Jack and Gwen, his hooded eyes sharp. 'Where? OK, keep the scene tight and the public out. I'm on my way.'

Watching him flip the lid shut, Gwen knew what he was going to say before the words were out.

'We've got another one.'

Outside, the heavens opened.

SEVEN

Adrienne Scott stared out at the rain that smeared itself against the other side of the reinforced window, distorting her reflection. Her left eye slid lazily downwards towards her nose, turning its elegantly made-up oval into a sagging circle, whilst her right stared into itself and at the drooping bag underneath that expensive face creams could no longer hold back. She looked hard and ugly. The stylish bob that had cost her a fortune was too sharp, removing any softness from her angular face. Great in the courtroom, perhaps not so great for getting along in the real world. Perhaps this was her true reflection.

Bad mother.

The drops outside grew heavier, smashing silently into the reinforced glass, and her alter ego's mouth trembled for a moment before blending with her chin. Maybe this was the way Ryan saw her: an ugly monster to be avoided. In some ways she wished that were true. At least if he saw her as a beast, it would indicate that she had some presence in his life, other than just as an irritant like all the other people he was forced to have some kind of interaction with. Adrienne knew better than that, though. In a small, dead part of her heart, she knew that she was nothing to Ryan. Not even a concept. She was as intangible as the transparent reflection that tried in vain to stay solid in the window.

Behind her, Ryan had slipped directly from 'Walking In The Air' into 'Where Is Love?' from the musical *Oliver!* Even with Ceri trying to cajole a drink of water into his mouth, each note held its purity, fluidly shifting from one to the next. As always when her boy sang, the haunting emotional quality he created with his voice made it almost impossible for anyone seeing him for the first time to really believe he could be so disconnected from people. No one could sing like that without some huge reservoir of emotion bursting through their skin, surely?

In the early days, which were only a few years ago, but seemed and felt like a lifetime to Adrienne, some of his singing would make her cry all night. Even after he'd moved in permanently to the Havannah Court centre, she would go home to the wreck of her marriage and curl up on her side of the bed and wait for the snoring to start so she could let the less beautiful sound of her own pain out to be poured wetly into her pillow. His voice would haunt her more than the deadness of his intelligent expression and for a long while she was convinced that it was an indication of his trapped feelings. He *did* love and need her; he just didn't know how to express it. She didn't care what the doctors said. She was his mother. She *knew*. She wanted more tests. More evaluations. They'd all got it wrong.

It was only when Michael had dragged her into Ryan's room, the little boy oblivious to the rage of his parents as they screamed at each other, and forced her to listen to him – to really listen to him – and then to listen again to that damned CD, that the truth hit home. She finally saw it. Or heard it. Whichever. Her heart broke for the final time that day, all her hopes and dreams of one day reaching her blond angel, shattered in the music. Michael and the doctors had been right all along. All the beautiful power in Ryan's voice was just the original singer's emotion *made better*. It was as if her tiny, talented, lost child was a mechanical computer. He absorbed the sound and reproduced it, but as it should be. The perfect version. He had enhanced the song, but not with his own emotions, whatever they were.

Michael had been right, but she couldn't forgive him for it. That day was the last time she had spoken to him. Perhaps it wasn't only Ryan that could be so remote. And the advantage of being one of Cardiff's best barristers meant that the divorce was swift and clean-cut. Their marriage was executed as painlessly as possible.

'Bloody awful weather, isn't it?' Ceri's soft voice broke Adrienne's reverie and she turned round. The nurse was trying to slip a baby's drinking bottle of fruit juice into Ryan's mouth. 'I was hoping we'd get one of those Indian summers.' Ceri looked up, her round face cheerful, despite having to catch the mouthfuls of juice that dribbled down the little boy's chin. 'You know, the kind that the people on the weather are always telling us to expect but never arrive.'

Adrienne gave her a tired smile. 'I know the kind.'

Ryan sat unmoving on the bed, his blue eyes staring into some void that only he understood, his mouth still producing the music in spite of the bottle being gently pushed into the corner of his mouth. Adrienne didn't know how his voice hadn't totally given out or been damaged by now. But then Ryan was the only child in the unit who would sleep for twelve-hour stretches every night, regular as clockwork. Maybe twelve hours on and twelve hours off was what his body needed. Adrienne often thought that those twelve hours where Ryan was completely lost in the darkness of his own mind must be his favourite times. If he was capable of such things as favourites. The workings of little Ryan Scott's mind and heart were truly an enigma.

'Didn't you have a holiday this year?' Adrienne asked, pretending to ignore the juice that slipped down her son's tiny Welsh rugby shirt. She never came at meal times. She just didn't have the stomach for it – one more indication of her uselessness to a boy like Ryan.

'No.' Ceri caught the liquid stream before it made its way to the carpet. 'My mum's waiting for a hip operation so I've been looking after her when I can. Didn't want to leave her.' She gave Adrienne a warm, open, beaming smile. 'I can always dream of booking myself some winter sun, but I expect I'll just wait for next year to roll around and grab myself two weeks in Magaluf, the same as everyone else.'

Leaning against the window sill, Adrienne allowed her own expression to soften for a minute. They were chatting as if it were perfectly normal for a little boy to be singing over their conversation while ignoring the toys that remained in the same place every day because he really had no use for them.

'You're looking after your mother as well?' Adrienne let out a sigh. 'I don't know how you do it, Ceri.'

'It's not so much. I just do her shopping and that kind of thing.' The nurse looked up and Adrienne hated seeing the care and concern there. Her natural defences growled and sprang into position, forcing her to straighten her back a little and set her face in a frown as if she were in the middle of a particularly tricky cross-examination.

Ceri watched her for a moment, and Adrienne had an idea that she was used to breaking through barriers far tougher than Adrienne could provide.

'What you do is harder.' Ceri paused and looked sadly at Ryan. 'He's so far locked inside himself nothing will ever touch him I don't think, no matter what we try.'

'I just wish he'd bloody shut up.' The thought escaping before she had time to tame it, Adrienne was shocked by the harsh bitterness of her own voice.

Ceri nodded a little. 'I can understand that. It's so beautiful.' She wiped away more juice and sat her solid body back on her heels. 'But it's only automatic. I doubt he even hears it, that's what Doctor Chipra says. He says he sings to protect his silence. To keep the sounds of the world away from him.' Ceri ran a hand over the boy's blond hair with a gentle affection that made Adrienne envious.

'Poor little mite.'

Adrienne watched them for a moment longer and wished she could find something other than hollow sadness in her heart.

TORCHWOOD

EIGHT

Having spent the whole day so far inside the Hub trying to make some sense of the Rift data, Ianto wouldn't have known if it was raining, snowing or the middle of a heatwave up on Cardiff's pavements if it hadn't been for the dampness of Gwen's hair. He was beginning to feel like a Weevil stuck underground all the time. Carrying the coffees, he went to join Jack and Gwen in the Boardroom. Maybe not a Weevil. At least they got to go out and wreak some havoc at night time. He was more like a mole. Yes, analysing all the data was important, but it seemed that the only time he had been allowed out on the surface recently was to pick up the pizza.

'OK, let's see what we've got.' Standing at the end of the table, Jack spread the images of the bodies across its surface.

Ianto took his usual seat and, seeing that Gwen had done the same, immediately wished he'd broken the habit. The empty chairs between them throbbed, and Ianto was sure that however much the three of them talked, the lost voices that should fill them would still be heard the loudest in their absence. Sipping his coffee, and letting it burn his throat, he focused on Jack.

'Three people dead in the space of just over twelve hours.' As Jack spoke, a map of the Cardiff area came up on the screen behind him. Three red dots stood out. 'As you can see, none of them were that close to each other, but there were spikes of Rift activity just before each death, so we know we're most likely dealing with something alien.'

Ianto looked at the photographs on the table for a moment. 'Who was the third victim?'

'Karen Peters.' Gwen pulled her wet hair back into an untidy ponytail. 'She died at eleven o'clock this morning at the Cooper Drake Insurance office where she worked.'

'At work? So we've got some reliable witnesses then?'

Gwen shook her head, and Jack cut in. 'Like the other two, Miss Peters was an amateur singer. She was in the bathroom practising alone when she died.'

'Tiled rooms are good for acoustics,' Ianto muttered, peering at a photo of the woman, thankfully taken when she'd been very much alive and all her insides were still where they should be. He put Karen Peters at maybe mid-thirties and decided she would probably have been attractive if it wasn't for the slightly surly look in her eyes and the thinness of her smile. He doubted, if this picture was anything to go by, that she had been particularly popular amongst the workers at Cooper Drake's. Sometimes faces said more than words ever could.

'The acoustics certainly kicked in when she started screaming. Apparently the sound carried straight into the air vents. The man who found her thinks it was only maybe three minutes from when he first heard her to his getting into the bathroom.' Jack raised an eyebrow. 'Given the sounds that were coming out of there, he didn't knock and wait.'

'So, whatever it is, it works fast.' Gwen leaned back in her chair. 'Three minutes to open someone up and take their vocal cords. That's got to be more fiddly than just ripping out someone's liver or another obvious organ.'

Jack smiled. 'It sounds like someone's been taking a sneaky look at that anatomy chart.'

'Ha bloody ha.'

'So how did it get in?' Ianto felt as if he were playing catch up. Getting the information second hand was never quite the same as actually being there. 'Past security? Surely that would mean it would have to be able to pass for human.' He looked from Jack to Gwen and back to Jack again. If that was the case then they were really in trouble.

'No.' Jack shook his head. 'A small skylight against the outside wall was smashed. It got in that way.'

'The bathroom window at the bed and breakfast was broken too,' Gwen added. 'And that was the only way the alien could have got to Barry Llewelyn without going past his wife.' She looked at Jack.

Ianto frowned. Why did he get the feeling he was missing something? 'It came through the stained-glass window of the church too. So it comes through glass windows instead of using the door.' He shrugged. 'Aliens have done stranger things.' His memory raced back through all the events of the past few years. 'A *lot* stranger.'

Jack shook his head, but it was Gwen who spoke. 'The church window was huge, but the bathroom windows at both the B & B and Cooper Drake's were tiny. Only something the size of a small child could get through the space.'

'So we're looking for a small alien that's good at getting to high spaces?'

Jack nodded. 'Or something that can change its shape or molecular structure at will. Which would make more sense given how the victims' skin and clothes – the two that were wearing any, that is – were somehow fused to become one.'

'That must narrow it down.'

Hands on his hips, Jack laughed a little. 'You have no idea how many species there are that can do amazing things with their forms. The human body is pretty damned inflexible compared to what can be found out there, and that's only in *our* galaxy.'

'I don't know.' Ianto kept his expression deadpan. 'The human body has its moments.'

'Yes, and we do have the glory of both male and female to enjoy.' Jack's grin was infectious, the mood lightening for a moment.

'For some of you maybe, Captain Harkness,' Gwen joined in. 'Most of us pick one or the other and stick with it.'

'Really, PC Cooper? Speaking of aliens, I remember the time when you first joined us and that particularly frisky female in the cells…'

'Let's focus on the alien at hand, shall we?' Gwen cut in, glaring playfully at Jack. 'What else have we got to go on?'

Still smiling a little, Jack looked from Ianto to Gwen. 'You two tell me.'

'OK,' Gwen started. 'They're all singers.'

'They're all *good* singers,' Ianto added. 'Probably among the best in the competition. I haven't checked the third victim yet, but the others have all finished in the top three of their category at some point over the past four years.'

'Karen Peters did too,' Jack said. 'Came third two years ago. Didn't compete last year because of a strained throat and didn't want to finish badly.'

'And the alien takes the instruments they use to sing with.'

'But why?' Gwen asked. 'Because it likes the sound or because it hates it?'

Jack rested his hands on the desk and leaned on it. 'Right at the moment that doesn't matter. What's important is that the singing somehow draws it.'

'But why now? This competition has been running for a few years now. Why hasn't the alien attacked earlier?'

'The competition's much bigger this year than before.' Ianto looked up. 'Don't you read the local papers? Just about every spare space in Cardiff has been rented out to choirs and singers from all over Wales. After *Britain's Got Talent*, they all seem to think they're going to be the next Paul Potts. That or the last choir standing.' He sipped his coffee, shaking his head slightly. 'Everyone seems to suddenly think they can sing their way to fifteen minutes of fame, but at least in this competition you have to get past the regional heats. And even though a lot more have got through from those this year, most of the worst ones will get knocked out in the final rounds.'

It was only when he paused that Ianto noticed both Gwen and Jack staring at him.

'What?'

Gwen felt the corners of her mouth tugging into an amused smile. 'Just sounds like you know a lot about it, that's all.'

Ianto frowned. Why did he suddenly feel like he'd admitted to something weird? 'I used to do a bit of singing myself.' He paused, trying but failing miserably to keep the defensive edge out of his voice. 'In fact, I've picked up tickets for the final. It'll be nice to be *in* the Millennium Centre for once, rather than under it.'

Jack smiled. 'Two tickets?'

'Of course.'

Gwen was still staring at him as if he had something

strange smeared across his face and she didn't know quite how to address it. But then she could be like that. Just because she had the most obvious 'real' life out of the Torchwood team, both past and present, Ianto thought she sometimes forgot that they'd all had lives of some sort before joining up, and sometimes ghosts from them lingered. And not all of the ghosts were bad.

'A singer,' Gwen said finally. 'I wish I'd known that earlier. You could have sung at mine and Rhys's wedding. It would have been lovely.'

Ianto smiled. 'Don't you think your wedding day was special enough?'

'You're right.' Gwen sighed. 'I was bloody lucky to make it down that aisle at all. Wouldn't have wanted you distracted by trying to remember a load of lyrics. And anyway, after all that running around you'd have probably sounded crap anyway.'

All three of them back in the memory for a moment, Ianto watched as Jack's eyes dropped to the empty chairs. For a moment they sat in silence, but Ianto didn't feel the need to break it. No one needed to speak, and he was pretty sure that none of them had the words anyway.

Eventually, Jack coughed a little. 'So, we've got an alien that is drawn to good singing for whatever reason, and can change shape and move freely over high spaces. At least it's a start. Gwen, I want you to do a database search on the last two criteria. When you're done, give me what you've found and I'll take over. That sound thing is bugging me.'

Gwen nodded. 'What about the press? Are you going to give Cutler a cover story he can use for now? I don't see three mutilated singers staying off the front pages, no matter how many strings you pull.'

'Cutler's a big boy. He can manage for now. And anyway, I'm not sure I want this kept quiet at the moment. If it frightens a few singers away, there's not so many left for us to worry about. Speaking of which…' He glanced down at that large dial of his watch. 'I think it's time for the news.'

Out of the Boardroom and back in the heart of the Hub, Jack, Gwen and Ianto gathered around the small TV that looked so out of place amongst the high-tech computer equipment that filled the desk spaces. Jack turned the volume up as the opening titles for the news came to an end, then folded his arms across his chest.

The murders were the first headline, and Ianto thought that if Jack was happy for the press to be involved in this one then he should be looking pretty ecstatic. The newsreader stared intently into the camera.

'*Three competitors in the Welsh Amateur Operatic Contest have been found dead in three separate locations across the city over the past twenty-four hours. The victims, two male and one female, whose names have not been released, were all qualifiers for this year's final to be held in ten days' time at Cardiff's Millennium Centre. Although the police are not releasing any details of the causes of death, it is believed that they are treating each as a murder enquiry and have not ruled out that the deaths are linked.*'

The camera cut away from the studio and out to Cardiff's central police station. A tired-looking blond man in his thirties came out of the building and stopped at the top of the stone steps. He didn't carry an umbrella, instead ignoring the rain as he stared grimly into the flashing bulbs and microphones of the journalists.

'Is that Cutler?' Ianto asked.

Jack nodded. 'Does his face ring any bells?'

Ianto shook his head. 'Should it?'

'He says he had a case that was taken over by Torchwood One back in 2003. You used to work there. Dig through the records we've got and see if you can find out what it was. I'm curious. He seems pretty sharp.'

Ianto nodded. 'Will do.'

On screen, Cutler glared at the camera, his chin tucked down a little, like a boxer preparing for a fight, as journalists shouted questions over each other. After a moment, he raised his hand, his brow furrowing slightly with impatience. He didn't wait for the small crowd to fall silent but started speaking over them, forcing their quiet if they wanted to hear what he had to say.

'We obviously can't say too much at this time given that the investigation is under way, but South Wales Police can confirm that three bodies have been found dead over the past twenty-four hours, and that we are treating these deaths as suspicious.' He paused, the space immediately filled with a cacophony of voices all demanding attention. Cutler continued as if only he and the camera were present.

'We also have reason to suspect that the deaths may be linked. Until we can give out further information, we would ask the public not to panic but also to take the usual sensible precautions.' For the first time he lifted his chin fully. 'That's all I can say at this time.'

Turning, Cutler moved quickly away from the reporters who were still shouting questions at him and went back into the station. Ianto was pretty sure he could make out words like 'Singers' and 'Competition' in the questions fired at the policeman's back. Given the way the victims had died, he figured it wouldn't be too long before one of the tabloids was hinting at the gruesome details, no matter how much of a media ban the police put on them, and then there'd be panic. As much as working for Torchwood was sometimes draining, he didn't envy Cutler's job.

Jack rolled up his sleeves and clapped his hands. 'Right then, let's get to work. We've got an alien to track down.'

NINE

Up on the Cardiff streets, evening slowly drew in, the dark night falling with the rain, coating the gloom with shifting shadows. Heels clicked quicker on the pavements, as people rushed to find their way to the warmth of their bright homes, shivering away the dampness of the day. Cars and buses blared horns and churned out chunks of acrid, irritated fumes. No one looked up. And, even if they had, the dark shape that darted here and there against the night would have been barely visible as it searched the city.

Hannah Lafferty undid the buttons of her smart woollen coat and gritted her teeth. The woman had to be joking. Beside her, the rest of the Milford Haven Women's Institute Choir were doing exactly as she was, all staring in disbelief at their musical director, Annaliese George. Hannah's fingers resisted the stiff buttons and, glancing down, she didn't recognise the gnarled hand at the end of her wrist for a moment. When did all those knotted veins and liver spots appear? Why was it that sometimes slow changes seemed to happen all of a sudden? Was it supposed to fool you into thinking that old age was somehow OK?

Feeling the numbness that had been rattled into the base of her spine since the early morning, Hannah decided that her hand was attached to the right body. A body that was getting old and couldn't deny it any longer. Her stare intensified into a glare as the choir and its director moved into a silent stand-off. It had been a fairly long journey in a very old minibus with only a tired fan heater on the dashboard to keep them warm, and none of their joints were as young or flexible as they used to be. Even Alice Jones, who was a mere slip of a thing at only 45, had complained of a sore back when they'd finally climbed out at the hotel.

And the hotel was another story in itself. After deciding to give the competition a whirl, admittedly at Annaliese's insistence, and having surprised themselves by getting through the regional heats, they had been very pleased with themselves when they had booked their accommodation early. No one would be able to say the Women's Institute was disorganised and left with nowhere to stay, not like some of the larger choirs in the competition whose members had ended up scattered far and wide in hotels and bed and breakfasts across the city because they'd left their bookings too late.

However, as they'd gathered in the tatty and cramped reception area, it had become all too apparent that the Melrose Hotel didn't live up to the photos and description on its website. Hannah's teeth clenched tighter, straining her jaw, which wouldn't be good for her singing, but she couldn't help that. The hotel had failed to mention in their advertising that they had no lift, that all ten of the ladies' twin rooms were up on the fourth floor, and that the stairs were steep and uneven to say the least. Some doctors might encourage old women to spend their days dragging themselves up and down flights of steep and uneven stairs for no good reason other than their health but, as far as 62-year-old Hannah Lafferty was concerned, those doctors were daft. Old age was all about taking it easy and eating what you wanted. If it had been up to her, they'd have complained to the manager, but it seemed the rest of the group didn't want to cause a fuss and so she had gone along with it.

Staring now at Annaliese George and her chignon hair and perfect make-up, Hannah decided this was one time she was going to take a stand.

'What exactly do you mean you want us to move all the chairs?' Her voice a soft growl, she felt very tempted to point out that Annaliese was quite new to the organisation and should really stop trying to boss them around. She was their musical director; she could boss them around when they were singing. That was about it.

'They'll interfere with the acoustics.' Annaliese's clipped tones reeked of Surrey, and Hannah wished, not for the first time, that the woman would just move back there.

Enid Evans timidly stepped up, unwinding a scarf from around her neck. The corner of her mouth twitched slightly. 'But there must be at least a hundred or more of them.'

'Keep that scarf on, Enid!' Annaliese tutted. 'You need to protect your voice.'

'Well, folding up and stacking all those chairs is hardly going to help our singing voices, is it?' Alice's voice rose from somewhere towards the back of the group, and Hannah smiled. The choir had no chance of winning anything in the competition, they had no illusions about that, but they did have Alice Jones and her beautiful soprano. Some of the others might not want to admit it, but it was Alice who lifted them out of the ordinary and into something more than that.

'*You* don't have to move them, Alice.' Annaliese obviously knew it too. 'You could just make sure that everyone has a bottle of water to sip by their place.'

A murmur of discontent rustled along the line, and Hannah raised an eyebrow. 'We don't have any stars in the choir, Annaliese.'

'No we don't,' added Alice.

Hannah stared at the rows of chairs that stretched towards the gloomy rear of the Llandaff community centre, and then checked her watch. 'Look ladies, we've only got the hall for an hour and a half. It's six o'clock now. If we move all those chairs it'll just waste rehearsal time. We can work around the acoustics. Let's just get on with singing.'

The rustle of discontent translated into murmurs of assent and, knowing when she'd lost, Annaliese clapped her hands together and turned her back on the uniform chairs. 'Let's get to your places and ready to start. Form your lines.' With a nod and a raised eyebrow she organised the choir into a presentable semi-circle of three rows. 'And remember ladies, never sing louder than lovely!'

Half an hour later and they were in full voice, belting out their arrangement of 'How Do You Solve A Problem Like Maria?' It had been Annaliese's choice and, although Hannah had hated it at first, she had to admit that it worked for them. They were women of the right age and could have fun with it, without making it sound twee. As much as Annaliese George irritated her as a person, she was definitely a talented musical director.

Despite the chill that hovered under the high ceilings of the practical seventies hall, Hannah's face was warm as her breath moved in a steady flow, pushing out her sections of the song, and she relaxed into the enjoyment of being part of the wave of sound created by her friends around her. She looked down at Annaliese, her stout but elegant form standing about two rows back into the empty audience seating, the top of her hair lost and absorbed into the dusky darkness of the rear of the centre.

Hannah tried not to smile, knowing that their musical director would pick it up immediately. Annaliese had insisted they leave the back lights off in order to create a theatre atmosphere since the chairs were already laid out. She said it would help them with their stage fright. Hannah thought they could turn out all the lights and she'd still have a hard time imagining she was on the stage of the Millennium Centre. Her stomach knotted for a second with a fizz of excitement. It was hard to believe they'd really made it this far.

Alice's voice cut through the air with the purity of a diamond through ice, and Hannah paused for breath, just relishing the exquisiteness of it. For a brief second though, something discordant interrupted it. Tilting her head, she peered at Annaliese, thinking she may have dropped a glass or bottle, but the conductor was smiling as she waved her arms and counted the next part in. That was strange. She was sure the sound had come from somewhere towards the back of the hall. Maybe she'd just imagined it. Taking a deep breath to come in with her section of altos, she stopped midway as Alice lost her note, veering into a bad sharp.

Annaliese rapped her baton harshly on the metal chair beside her, bringing the choir to an abrupt silence. She flashed an angry glare at Alice. 'What on Earth was that? You sounded like a cat that's been run over and left for dead.' Her mouth tightened into a thin line, all her hidden years apparent in the sudden crinkles around her lips. 'We can't have that so close to the finals. We're going to be on television, Alice. We're representing Women's Institute branches all over the country.'

Alice lifted her shoulders helplessly. 'I'm sorry. I don't know what came over me. I just felt...' She hesitated. 'I just felt a little strange for a moment.'

Hannah looked across at her younger friend. She was pale and trembling slightly. That didn't look like 'strange' to Hannah. That looked like fear. What could have shaken her like that?

'Maybe we should take a short break,' she said softly. 'I could use a quick drink of water.'

It was only when they were wearily leaving an hour later, that Enid spotted the pane of broken glass in the window beside the door. The group huddled round it.

'Was that here when we arrived?' Hannah stared at it. 'I thought I heard something breaking. Just before Alice lost that note. Must have been kids mucking around.'

With a big sigh, Annaliese hurried them outside and towards the battered minibus. 'The caretaker will be here in a minute to lock up. I'll explain it to him. I'm damned if they're going to charge us for the damage.'

Wearily, the women hauled themselves onto the minibus and waited in the damp chill for their conductor to join them, Hannah already looking forward to the four-storey climb to her bed. It had been a very long day.

The creature hung suspended somewhere at the edge of the dark space that had carried it so far from its origin, a void within a void, blackness coated in dark. It was too tired to pull itself into a physical form and it felt defeated. Feelings, emotions, the curse it carried: the creature endured them all in its silence. Too much loneliness. It had been pulled across the universe to this place, through the yawning cut in space and time that had found it desolate and alone and teased it with the noise of a different world; a world of sound, of communication, of emotion. It needed some of that. It needed to take this world home, to make its life bearable.

The shapeless form howled silently with frustration, the emotion a vibration across its surface. It was failing. It couldn't get what it wanted. The absorbed parts worked only on a barely functional level, reproducing primitive sound when the creature forced them to work, mentally manipulating the parts as if they were a mechanism but, however it tried, it couldn't make the air resonate and fill and touch its emptiness in the way that they did in their original hosts. Rage filled it and it came as bursts of cymbals and drums and soaring rich song in the alien's head. Until the sounds had come through the tear in the sky, it had only ever known empty silence, and now it couldn't bear to give those sounds up. It wouldn't go back, it couldn't, not until it could take the sound with it.

And so, after blinking in and out of the city seeking in vain, it waited, nothing at the edge of nothing, until the voices called it again.

TEN

After the short drive from the Millennium Centre to
Mermaid Quay, Maria Bruno, or plain Mary Brown as
she had been christened not so very many miles from
here, waited until Martin was ready with the umbrella
and then stepped out of the well-polished modern black
Sedan and walked elegantly into the five-star St David's
Hotel. She didn't acknowledge her supposed manager
and unfortunate husband as he scurried beside her,
holding the umbrella to make sure her perfectly set hair
didn't get wet. Perhaps that was all he was really good for,
being the hired help.

She fought an itch of irritation that threatened to force
its way onto her face. It never did to show one's feelings.
If only she'd realised Martin's limitations in their early
days. But then, they'd been caught up in the flush of love,

hard as that was to remember now, and who ever doubts the objects of their desire? All women want to believe their men strong and capable. Just like the heroes and lovers in the operas that she'd spent so much of her life performing.

The sleek doors slid open, and she stepped into the lobby holding her head high and back straight, flicking her wrist at Martin to shoo him and his umbrella away from her side. The bright lights bathed on her face and she pushed her chin out ever so slightly in order to make any lines on her neck less defined. Every entrance to every room was like an entrance on stage for Maria Bruno. She was a star, and for stars there were always people watching. If only these so-called celebrities would realise that these days. Then perhaps they'd remember to put their knickers on when they went out. The world had forgotten about class, and she intended to remind them of it.

Although she had to admit in her quieter moments, if only to herself, that some of those tasteless flash-in-the-pan pop stars had more fans than she did now. But she could blame that on Martin. He wasn't getting her the auditions she needed to keep herself on the premiere stages of Europe. Auditions. Even just thinking the word almost made her choke. Who would have thought that Maria Bruno, the finest soprano to come out of the Valleys, would have to audition for anyone. Until a few years ago, she had had to fight her way through the offers.

Her heart sinking a little, she forced her chin upwards to compensate. Dotted around the vast and clinical lobby a few heads turned her way, muttering amongst themselves with a buzz of recognition. A few pointed in her direction. It was barely surprising they knew who she was, even though she doubted any of them had ever heard her sing. Her face was on the posters for the competition that were spread on every billboard across the city. She pretended not to notice them. There was no class in acknowledging the fans. A cool aloofness was the way of true stars. And these weren't her fans, not really. They weren't the people who had waited outside the stage doors of the Royal Opera House on nights when Covent Garden had suffered worse rain than even Cardiff was getting, huddling there for hours just for a chance of getting an autograph. And yet here she was, judging a plebeian talent show simply in order to remind the world that she was still around. At least the final was being televised and she would be singing on it. That was something. Perhaps it would lead to an album deal. And the hotel was world class; she had to give the organisers credit for that. It seemed like a long time since she'd been pampered like this.

Her heels tip-tapping across the endless marble floor, she didn't pause as Martin struggled to take down the umbrella that'd had approximately thirty seconds' use.

'I'm going straight up. I'll see you in the morning.' She spoke without looking at him, focusing instead on pressing the button to call the elevator. 'Be a dear, and ask room service if they can send a fresh fruit salad up to me in half an hour.' If she looked at him he might see her disgust and pity and, as much as whatever love they had once shared was long gone, she didn't want him seeing that. He was mumbling something to her as, thankfully, the doors closed and the lift purred as it rose up through the atrium and to her suite on the fifteenth floor. It was bliss just to have a moment's peace.

An hour later and she'd soaked in the bath and nibbled the occasional piece of watermelon from the deliciously arranged fruit salad that the waiter had politely left on her table while she bathed. Having scrubbed her face clean, she reapplied a light base coat of make-up and a touch of natural pink lipstick and mascara. She wasn't planning on having visitors, but you never knew when someone might knock on the door and at ten o'clock it wasn't yet late enough to know that she'd be left undisturbed. Only just before turning out the final light would she let her skin sag as if it were letting out a long breath of air like any 52-year-old's would, even with regular Botox. Then she would reset her hair in curlers, before wrapping a scarf around her head and carefully going to sleep on her back. But for now, she'd stay casually glamorous.

Her open curtain lifted as a light breeze brushed past them and, picking up her champagne glass, Maria Bruno looked out onto the balcony and beyond. The air was cold and crisp and, after the heat of the bath, her skin prickled and tightened. It felt good. Sliding the doors open a little wider she stood in the opening, gazing out at the water, the moonlight dancing and winking back at her from its surface. She smiled a little, suddenly looking effortlessly younger than her years. It was beautiful. Wales was beautiful. At some point over the years she'd somehow forgotten that.

To her left, the lights of Cardiff Bay sparkled, the bars and restaurants staying valiantly vibrant despite the continual onslaught of dismal rain. If it weren't for the cold air, she could almost imagine herself somewhere on the Mediterranean. Her face tingled. But it was precisely the cold air that was giving the Bay its magical quality.

Closing her eyes, she pulled her diaphragm tight in a move that was as natural to her as breathing and, tilting her head back, none of the control for performing on stage required, she let her knees bend before the first delicate strains of 'Ave Maria' slipped from her mouth. Even though she was limiting her volume, the long notes soared out through the patio doors and into the night, carrying their beauty up to the freedom of the skies. For a moment, Maria herself was lost in the creation of the song, pouring her heart into it. When she performed this piece it was truly hers, her own 'Ave Maria': Ave Mary Brown, the poor girl made good.

The initial low notes fading away, she pulled herself up to the next octave, adding strength without damaging the emotional power or relaxing quality of the song. She needed no accompaniment other than the patter of rain on the balcony and, as the music filled the empty space

89

between the earth and the heavens, the haunting Latin words defied any who called the language dead.

'Et in hora mortis nostrae.'

And in our hour of death. She repeated the line three times, each time with more intensity than the one that went before. It was the song she wanted for her own cremation, preferably one of her own versions of it. Somewhere behind the music that filled her, soothing her as no other lover ever had, she wondered bitterly if Martin would manage to get that right.

A gust of sharp wind tugged her hair, and the temperature dropped suddenly. Stepping back slightly into the warm brightness of the room, Maria shivered, pulling her robe a little tighter across her body. Lowering her song to barely more than a whisper, she drew the sliding door shut. Maybe there was something to be said for the Mediterranean after all. Turning away, she reached for the champagne to refill her glass. Her hand stopped halfway. *There was something outside. On the balcony. But it was impossible.* Her singing stopped completely. Toes gripping the soft carpet beneath them, Maria Bruno's legs trembled as fear clambered up them, its invisible limbs clutching at her heart.

She turned back to face the doors. Outside, the night had sunk to some colour beyond black. Even the light from her room seemed to be sucked into the darkness beyond the glass, her reflection wavering, as if something on the other side was pulling it away.

Tears pricked the backs of her eyes, her breath cold in

her lungs as if that darkness – *whatever was in that darkness* – was filling her up, oozing into her through the air. One hand fluttered instinctively to her throat, but her terror was wrapped in her head, not her voice. Her brain was emptying. Her soul was emptying, filling instead with nothing. She tried to gasp but no sound came out. Not nothing. Worse than nothing. She was being left with only *her*; only the very core of herself as if no one else had ever existed. It was desolation. Isolation. Her heartbeat faded until it was only a whisper and then the echo of that whisper.

Across the room, the phone by the bed taunted her from a distant universe away. Unreachable. Untouchable. *And what would she say if she could…* Her internal thoughts drained away, leaving her fumbling for lost words, language fleeing from within her back to the *outside* where it belonged.

The unnatural blackness on the other side of the patio doors slowly pulled into itself, the antimatter creating a dense form. Flecks of metallic gunmetal grey shone as a solid, almost human shape appeared pressed against the glass. Its hairless skull and face were slick with a sheen like a crackled glaze on dark ceramic; the surface of its naked body covered in a network of sharp interlocking lines that made it appear fractured, as if the casing could never hold the bleakness inside. Two points of laser light beamed crimson from small dark spaces in the centre of its oval head, just above the shapeless hole that had to be its mouth.

For a moment they stared at each other, Maria lost in the rage of the red streaks that pierced through the glass as if it wasn't there, preferring even that to the terrible loneliness that filled her. She gasped again, aware of the pitiful sound escaping her, feeling the vibration in her perfect throat, but unable to hear it.

The thing outside tore its head from side to side, the strange mouth stretching wider and wider until the gaping hole almost filled its head, and all Maria could see was the endless void of darkness within. The creature's scream echoed in the desolate cavern of Maria's soul and, after hearing it pour through her insides, Maria knew, as a sense without words, that she would never sing again. The awful isolation carried in that empty sound owned her now. Everything else was lost.

As it was, the thought was irrelevant. A moment later, the glass smashed and, as the creature came for her, it seemed to Maria that her own scream was endless in her head.

ELEVEN

'Are you sure you don't want me to stick around a while longer?'

Jack looked up from his desk to see Gwen, her leather jacket already zipped up to the neck and her keys in her hands.

'Wouldn't it just break your heart if I said yes?' He grinned at her, despite the cramp in his neck from poring through the results of the database search that she had given him.

'Don't know about break my heart, but Rhys might come and break your face.' She tossed her long hair over one shoulder. 'He's cooking coq au vin tonight.'

Jack raised an eyebrow.

'Don't even *think* it, Jack.' Gwen warned him. Leaning on the doorframe, she looked reluctant to go but, as much as Jack felt like he could use the company on what was shaping up to be a long and frustrating night of staring at information and still finding no answers, he knew Gwen had the one thing that should be protected at Torchwood. A real life.

He'd seen what they did for a living destroy too many people who'd not let themselves focus on the real world, the one that had given them life and that had existed for them long before they'd ever heard of the Rift or Weevils or Captain Jack Harkness. Sometimes it was too easy to allow the strangeness of the things they dealt with daily to outshine the bland beauty of normality. But it would be normality that kept them sane, and what they would have to go back to if they lived long enough. He glanced at his watch, almost surprised by the time.

'It's ten o'clock. He's cooking dinner now?'

'It may have taken him a while, but Rhys has finally worked out that we don't work normal hours. When I say I might be working a bit late, he knows not to expect me till about now.'

'You'd better not disappoint him then.'

Gwen lingered, a small line of concern furrowing her pale brow. 'You sure you'll be OK?'

Jack smiled. Gwen was more than a little bit addicted to Torchwood herself. Her wanting to stay was part concern and part that *need* to be at the centre of the excitement, even if there was nothing happening. He'd seen it in her face the first time she'd ever come into Torchwood's range, peering over the edge of that multi-storey car park at them, still just a uniformed police officer. She'd come a long way since then. But that curiosity had only intensified with all she'd been through. She was tough, and Jack liked her. He liked her a lot.

'I'll be fine. Look, Ianto got me pizza! I won't starve while you're nibbling on Rhys's coq au vin.' He winked as she rolled her eyes. 'And anyway,' he continued, shrugging as his eyes dropped to the pieces of paper spread across his desk, some with scribbled notes on, others printed from the computer, 'I need some quiet thinking time to try and get to the bottom of all this.'

Gwen's face darkened. 'Let's hope whatever it is takes the night off. We need to catch this one, Jack. And quickly.'

'And we will.' He hoped he sounded more confident than he felt. 'Now scoot.'

Slapping the side of the wall as a goodbye, Gwen turned and within a few moments Jack heard the thick door to the lift slide shut, leaving him alone in the Hub. He stood behind his desk, the silence threatening to suffocate him for a moment, as if he'd been entombed once again in an early grave.

Sitting down heavily, already frustrated with the work ahead, he rustled some papers and for a brief moment wished he had asked one of the others to stay for a while, if only to sleep as he worked. Just to have the comfort of knowing there was another living being close by.

He shook the feeling off. It was just self-indulgence and self-pity, neither of which traits Jack had any patience with. He knew only too well from experience that having people with him wouldn't ease his deep-seated loneliness. He was different and, however much his team loved him and respected him, he would never be one of them. He couldn't die. That changed the way people looked at you.

Involuntarily, he glanced through the glass and towards the stairs. The ground at the bottom had been scrubbed clean, but for him would always be crimson stained against the clinical white from where Toshiko had bled to death, gutshot and still intent on saving the rest of them. If he could have taken her death, he would have and, although both Gwen and Ianto knew this, he knew they also couldn't help but perceive him as different. Alien in his own right. In many ways he was a freak. He had the one thing that most humans envied, but to him it felt like an endless curse.

He stared at the screen and listened to the hum of silence.

Silence.

Blood beat faster through his eternal veins.

'Silence… Now there's a thing…' he muttered softly under his breath. All self-pity gone as soon as it had come, his fingers whirred over the keyboard, his sharp eyes peering up through his fringe, focused on the state-of-the-art flat-screen monitor.

What if… he wondered. *What if the stories were true…* With renewed vigour, his fingers punched at the keys.

Loneliness, isolation, sound, emotion, shape-shifting.

He typed the words into a new search, highlighting a space in the far reach of the universe on the on-screen map. He wasn't really sure that the race or even the planet existed; he'd only heard of them through rumour and legend. But if they did… If they actually did, then maybe he had a chance of figuring out what they were dealing with.

The untouched pizza grew cold as Jack worked, his eyes never leaving the screen. It was shaping up to be a long night.

TORCHWOOD

TWELVE

An hour later, as Captain Jack Harkness was letting his untouched pizza grow cold, forgotten on the far corner of his desk, Ben Pritchard and Drew Powell were having a quiet drink in the King's Arms. The old pub, tucked down one of the narrower side streets in an ancient part of the city, was unusually quiet. With so many people in Cardiff for the competition, either as participants or spectators, it should have been busier even though it was raining outside. There were just a few groups of subdued drinkers spread through the rambling building's nook-and-cranny rooms, the sorts of private spaces that wreckers and thieves would have gathered in a couple of hundred years back in the harbour town.

Ben's nose crumpled a little as they lifted their large glasses of Pinot Grigio from the long wooden bar. The

King's Arms was the kind of pub that not so long ago would have been filled with a low-hanging cloud of dirty grey smoke that customers would have to wade through to reach a seat and, although the cigarettes were gone and there had obviously been a fresh lick of paint applied at some point in the last year or two, Ben thought that if he breathed in hard enough the ghosts of all those dead Marlboro Lights and Benson & Hedges would dive gleefully into his lung cavity and fester there in the hope of birthing some kind of tumour. Or at least ruining his voice for a week or two. And there would be plenty in the competition who would be thankful for that.

The Pritchard and Powell duet had come a very close second in the previous year's final, and since then it seemed to Ben that all their spare time had been devoted to practice, practice, practice, especially as this year the final was going to be televised and who knew what that could lead to. Drew in particular was desperate to win. And if Drew was happy then Ben was happy. Which pretty much summed up the full thirteen years of their relationship.

'Come on.' Drew stepped away from the bar. 'Let's go through there and grab a seat.' He nodded towards an alcove with a few steps leading down from it. 'And let's hope they've got cushions.'

Following his partner's rotund form as he bustled through the empty space of the main bar as if there were a crowd pressing into him on all sides, Ben couldn't help but smile. They were chalk and cheese. Whereas Ben could easily pass as straight by all stereotypical standards, Drew was an outright diva. What was the point in simply walking when you could flounce? Why cry when you could wail? Still, Drew had the kindest heart he'd ever known, and as far as Ben was concerned enough talent to be as demanding as he liked. Drew might be hard work, but Ben loved him. And he loved Ben and all his staid sensibilities. It was as simple as that.

Down in the snug bar, Drew paused. 'Oh God.'

'What's the matter?' With Drew's wide rear blocking the narrow stairwell, Ben couldn't see round the corner.

Drew nudged him in the ribs. 'Look.' He stepped aside a little, pressing into the wall so Ben could get past. His heart sank. Angus Parker, Tony Lockley and the small crew of cronies they took everywhere with them were gathered round the largest table in the small lounge area. Judging by the number of empty glasses stacked up in the middle, they'd been there for quite some time.

'Do you want to go somewhere else?' Ben whispered, his feet already backing up the stairs. They'd only wanted one quiet relaxing drink before going back to the hotel for the night. It didn't look like it would turn out that way.

'Too late,' Drew hissed. And he was right. Angus Parker had spotted them, a leering grin spreading across his thin, handsome face.

'Evening, ladies.'

The table gave him a round of snorts and titters as applause for his wit. Ben sighed. He'd have thought that some people would get bored of their own homophobia.

In the case of Angus Parker and his constant digs, however, it never let up, and in his quieter moments Ben was inclined to believe the young man with the delicate bone structure protested too much.

'Evening.'

Ben kept it neutral and flashed a small smile before moving to a table in the far corner. It was away from the others but, as far as he was concerned, nowhere near distant enough. Drew had stayed where he was, centre stage in the middle of the small room. He lifted his free hand and rested it on a tilted hip, one eyebrow raising as his full lips pursed. He looked with distaste at the pile of glasses on the table.

'Not expecting to do very well this year, boys?'

Tony Lockley's eyes narrowed and, watching from the corner, Ben inwardly groaned. Their quiet drink was going to be totally ruined and it was going to be Drew's fault. Why couldn't he just let things alone? Why did he always have to take the bait?

'What do you mean?'

Drew tutted. 'All that alcohol isn't good for the vocal cords, you know that.' He sighed. 'You wouldn't catch *us girls* drinking ourselves stupid with so few days to go before the finals.' He turned on his heel, strolling over to join Ben at last. 'But then I suppose,' he sent the parting shot without looking back, 'if you've got no chance of winning then it doesn't really matter. Cheers!'

Ben glared at Drew as he sat down, his ample rear spilling over the sides of the bar stool.

'What?'

'You know what.' Ben kept his voice low. 'Why do you have to antagonise them like that? Couldn't you have ignored them just for once?'

Drew shrugged, his eyes wide and innocent. 'Backing down's not in my nature, that's all.'

'Well, sometimes I wish you'd just take into account what's in *my* nature. I just wanted a quiet drink and now you've ruined that.' Ben could feel the hot, angry glares they were drawing from the other singers and knew that the argument wasn't over yet.

Drew's brow furrowed, never happy to be told off. 'They started it.'

'But you didn't have to join in.' Ben's dark eyes glowing with irritation at the parent-child nature of their conversation, he wondered why he was bothering. It was a pointless argument. Drew was incapable of walking away from the likes of Lockley and Parker. Especially those two. They'd been niggling at each other for the past three years of the competition. If only Drew could see that the fact that every year they beat the other two was enough to put them in their place. He didn't need to get into slanging matches with them. But once again it was too late.

Drew took a sip of his wine and leaned forward, his back bristling slightly. 'Are they looking at us?' he asked. 'I can feel them staring.'

'Of course they're looking at us. What did you expect? Now please, just ignore them.' Ben took a long sip of the perfectly chilled Pinot Grigio, but couldn't take any enjoyment from it. He just wanted to finish his drink and get them both out of there before it got nasty. It wouldn't turn into a physical fight, that didn't worry him, but after thirteen years with Drew he knew that the man could stay up all night festering over a well-delivered barbed comment that wasn't his own, and Drew wasn't one to fester quietly.

'Us younger men can handle it,' Lockley called over. 'I suppose at your age you've got to take more care.' He paused. 'Especially carrying all that weight.'

Ben watched Drew prickle, his jaw clenching and fingers tightening on his wine glass until parts of his pink skin turned white on his knuckles. If there was a way to goad Drew, it was to mention his weight. He'd piled on the pounds over the past three years since turning thirty, there was no denying that. He always claimed it was a thyroid problem, but Ben knew it was just a mixture of contentment, a fondness for cream cakes and an aversion to the gym. Ben didn't mind, and he figured that if it really bothered Drew that much he'd do something about it.

'Yeah,' Angus Parker joined in. 'Good job the only way Ben has to carry you is in your singing. He'd never manage you over a threshold.'

This brought hoots of mirth from the other singing pair's small audience, which consisted of a man in his forties who was none too slim himself, a scrawny blonde who obviously had a crush on the handsome Angus, a brunette who Ben thought didn't look old enough to be in a pub in the first place – and her acne, however well she thought she'd hidden it beneath a thick layer of too dark make-up, was not persuading him otherwise – and an older man Ben recognised as Angus Parker's uncle, who worked as a kind of roadie for them. It made Ben smile. Angus and Tony wanted to be treated like pop stars but sang classical music. He'd never known two men less comfortable in themselves, but they wouldn't want to hear that from a 35-year-old, happily homosexual man.

The final jibe mocking his weight and his voice was too much for Drew to bear. He turned slowly on the stool until he was facing his antagonist.

'And where are you planning on coming this year? In the top five?' He snorted derisively. 'Let me just remind you that Pritchard and Powell came second last year and, if you must know, several bookies have us odds-on favourites to win the final. Some of us are actually *in* the competition. We're not just playing at it.' He paused dramatically. 'Who knows, after this we may even go professional. Whereas I doubt you two can even spell professional.'

Across the room, the laughing stopped and Ben could see the anger flaring up in the flush of both young men's faces. Drew could sound damned patronising at times, and this was one of those times.

'We're working-class men and proud of it,' Angus Parker's uncle growled from over the lip of his pint glass. Ben had never stood close enough to the man to find out, but he wouldn't have been surprised if he'd had 'love' and 'hate' in homemade tattoos on his knuckles. He looked like a man who'd had an interesting life.

'I'm sorry,' Ben cut in. 'He doesn't mean anything by it.'

Drew turned, his neck long and chin tilted upwards, and scowled. His displeasure was obvious.

'I'd rather be a proper bloke and working class than some middle-class poofter,' Angus sneered.

Without speaking to Ben, Drew returned his attention to the small crowd in the other room. A smirk twisted on his full mouth. 'A middle-class poofter that can sing you off the stage.' The smile turned into a grin. 'And I think, sweetheart,' he purred, 'it takes more than being common to make someone a proper bloke.' He winked. 'And from what I've heard, you've not got much in that department.'

Draining almost half his glass in one mouthful, Ben's mood darkened, as if a gauze veil had slipped down between him and the rest of the people in the pub. Tension tightened in his throat and his jaw clenched. What he needed was to relax. His singing would be awful otherwise. And as much as this argument might be over for Drew by morning, his own resentment would linger. He couldn't just let these things go like Drew did. Drew would be screaming at you one minute and crying with laughter the next, his dark moods coming and going as swiftly as a brief summer's downpour. Ben was different. Things *stayed* with him. And if he couldn't shake them, then his lungs and diaphragm seized up and lost power.

And if that happened this year then Drew really would have something to be upset about. Even after all their years together, Drew didn't really get how Ben was different to him. Drew thought that, underneath everything, all people were just like he was, with the exception perhaps of Angus Parker and Tony Lockley.

Lockley nudged Parker. 'Did you see on the news about those singers that got murdered?' His voice was loud. 'Maybe we should try and point whoever did it in Fat Boy's direction.' His laugh was like a pig's snort: animal and unpleasant. 'Get him out of all our hair.'

'I bet the whole bloody competition would chip in to pay for that.' Blonde girl's words slurred slightly. 'I've only had to listen to him for five minutes and he's doing my head in.'

Both Parker and Lockley laughed aloud at that, and Ben wearily wondered which one of the two she would have the pleasure of shagging that night, and whether she'd even remember it in the morning. Suddenly, the whole place turned sour and seedy in his mind's eye. He finished the rest of his wine.

'Are you going to let them speak to me like that?' Drew stared at him, his chin wobbling slightly.

'They're drunk. Forget it.' Ben stood up. 'I'm going.'

'What do you mean you're going? I haven't finished my drink yet.'

'Well, I have.' He paused, keeping his simmering anger locked in the tightened muscles of his jaw. 'I don't need this, Drew. You knock yourself out with these wastes of space, and I hope it makes you feel better. Me? I'm going to get some fresh air.'

Without waiting for a reply, Ben strode over to the alcove and up the stairs to the main bar, ignoring the catcalls of 'Get her!' that followed him. He wasn't angry with Parker and Lockley. They were what they were. He was angry with Drew for always needing to win.

He didn't have to turn round to know that Drew was coming after him, but it was only when he'd left the pub and was striding along the narrow cobbled street in no particular direction other than *away* that Drew finally called after him.

He turned and stared at the chubby man standing helplessly in the pub doorway.

'What?'

The few metres between them seemed too vast for either to cross, and Drew must have sensed it because he hesitated where he was rather than coming forwards.

'I'm sorry!' he called. 'I really am. I'm an idiot.' His hands fluttered as he spoke. 'I'm sorry.' He repeated the words more softly, as if for the first time he realised just how annoyed Ben was.

'You always are. But it doesn't stop you doing it again.'

'Let's go somewhere else and have a drink. I'll be perfect. I promise.'

Ben looked at the ground rather than at Drew. If he looked into his partner's hangdog expression then he'd only feel guilty about being angry, and that would make him more angry. He sighed. He just needed half an hour on his own.

'Go back to the hotel,' he said finally. 'I'll see you back there in an hour or so.' Turning his back, he strode away.

'Ben!'

Not looking round, Ben raised one arm in a half-hearted wave goodbye and then thrust his hands deep into his pockets, hunching over a little to keep warm. At least the rain had eased to a drizzle, the water a fine mist, teasing his skin. He sped up a little, enjoying the air filling his lungs, the exercise helping shake away the tension that squeezed at his insides.

Eventually the narrow road opened out into a more modern boulevard, large 1930s semi-detached houses uniformly lining one side, and a vast park filling the other. From the glow of the street lamps on the residents' side, he could just make out a children's play area close to the pavement. Smiling, he followed the green iron-railing fence until he reached the small entrance and stepped inside. For a moment, he cautiously peered across the softly sprung area. A see-saw was a mere grey shadow in the gloom, and the swings tilted backwards and forwards slightly on the breeze, the chains creaking like old joints. The roundabout was silently still. There was no one there; no drunks or junkies or kids waiting for some hapless passer-by to pick on or kick in.

He was alone.

The ground mute beneath him, he padded to the swings and sat in the middle of the three, leaving the other two empty to be filled by whatever ghosts of children danced in them in the night. The chains pressed into his hips, but he didn't mind. His knees bending slightly, he pushed himself back and then lifted his legs to let the seat do what it was designed to do.

Drifting backwards and forwards, he stared out into the inky blackness of the park. The gentle motion helped ease the tightness in his shoulders. Shutting his eyes, he let the damp air slide slowly in and out of his lungs, each time the breath lasting for longer than the previous. Somewhere in the distance an owl hooted. In the invisible darkness a bush rustled.

When his lungs were relaxed, Ben began to sing.

THIRTEEN

Gwen lay in the crumpled mess of her bed, her legs tangled in the warm sheets that Rhys had just vacated, and grinned sleepily. Her thighs tightened as if it were still her husband they were wrapped around. She really was a lucky girl. She couldn't believe it had taken her so long before she'd realised it.

Beside her a cup of coffee was cooling, and from the bathroom she could hear Rhys humming badly as he brushed his teeth. She stifled a giggle. She couldn't even figure out the tune amidst the sound of the tap running and the scrubbing of his toothbrush that were not helping Rhys's general tendency towards being completely tone deaf. There was no need to worry about some alien coming and ripping him open for his vocal cords.

Although the thought had slipped frivolously into her

head, her face darkened. She didn't want to think about the deaths of yesterday. It was only seven o'clock. She had an hour before she had to be at the Hub. One more hour of relative normality.

'Hey you!' Rhys paused his tuneless serenade, calling to her through the open bathroom door as the power shower burst into life. 'They keep telling us we're in a recession. How about we save on the water bill and you jump in here with me?'

Kicking back the covers, Gwen laughed. They'd had a pretty good date night, even after everything she'd seen yesterday. The food was brilliant, and everything that came after was pretty fabulous too. Despite the problems they'd had in their relationship when she first started at Torchwood, since they'd been married they'd rarely argued. Maybe part of that was to do with Owen and Tosh's deaths, and when she thought she'd lost Rhys himself. She wasn't going to risk that pain again. She still felt a wave of guilt tingeing her sadness when she thought of Owen and how she'd betrayed Rhys with him. It had been crazy and she wished she'd never done it, but it was all over now. She had to let it go, along with Owen himself.

'Well?' Rhys's throaty, dependable Welsh voice pulled her back from the dark memories of the past.

'I'm just coming.'

Sitting up, she took a gulp of her coffee before pushing the covers back and getting up. Stretching lithely, and feeling very much like the cat that got the cream, she decided there were worse ways to start the day. She'd taken four steps towards the bathroom when her mobile rang, and the metaphorical cream suddenly went off. Only work would be calling her at this time in the morning. In fact, as her time with Torchwood had gone on, it seemed that her mobile only ever rang if it was Rhys asking when she'd be home or Jack, Ianto, Tosh or Owen asking when she'd be getting her butt to the Hub. And now she was left with the fifty-fifty of whether it was Jack or Ianto.

'Hang on. My phone's going!' she shouted, hoping her husband would hear over the shower and his bad singing, as she dived across the bed to answer it. The caller ID showed it was Ianto.

'What's happened?' Before the words were even out of her mouth, she instinctively knew the answer. The alien had claimed another victim in the night. Dammit. Her stomach clenched and the memory of her lovely evening with Rhys was permanently soured. She should have been working. They all should have been.

'Watch the news. Then get to the Hub. Quickly.'

'I'm on my way.'

They hung up simultaneously without any of the niceties that society expected, and, with all thoughts of her shower gone, Gwen flicked the TV on and found the news channel. It was 7.15. Headline time.

'Maria Bruno, who left her natural home of Wales at 17 to find fame singing on all the finest stages of the world, was in Cardiff as part of the judging panel for the televised final of the city's annual Amateur Operatic

Contest. At the height of her success in the nineties, Bruno was considered one of the greatest sopranos in the world, regularly performing alongside such greats as the late Luciano Pavarotti.'

Pulling her T-shirt on, Gwen glared at the perfectly coiffed woman on the TV. Why couldn't she just get to the point?

'Her sudden death has come as a great loss to all who knew her and will be felt deeply in the world of opera where she brought so much joy. We hope to speak to one of her fellow judges shortly, but right now we're going over live to the St David's Hotel in Cardiff, where Judy Glover has been since the news broke.'

The newsreader turned in her chair to face the screen behind her, where the familiar sight of Mermaid Quay came into view and a young woman, who was trying desperately to ignore the drizzle trickling down her face, stared seriously into the camera.

'So, Judy,' the newsreader continued from the dry warmth of the studio. 'Are you able to shed any further light on the events surrounding Maria Bruno's death yet?'

Yanking on her jeans, Gwen paused. This was the important bit.

Rhys emerged from the bathroom, a towel wrapped around his waist. 'I thought you were coming to join—'

Without glancing at him, Gwen raised a hand to silence him. She needed to hear this. The bedsprings creaked as he sat beside her.

'Yes, I can.' The reporter on location looked grim. 'Obviously the police have yet to release a statement, but a source from inside the hotel has told us that Ms Bruno went to her suite at about nine o'clock last night and had some fruit salad delivered at nine-thirty. Her husband, Martin Meloy, who is also her manager, had a separate suite next door and he remained in the bar of the hotel until approximately half past eleven, when he returned to his own room. Ms Bruno was an early riser and her routine was that her breakfast was delivered to Mr Meloy who would then let himself into her suite and wake her with it.' The reporter paused. 'And it was when he did so that he discovered her body.'

'And do we have any possible details on what might be the cause of her death?'

A sock in one hand, Gwen stared at the TV.

'Well, as you can see from all the cars and vans behind me, there's a lot of police presence at this five-star hotel this morning and, although they have yet to release a statement, sources within the hotel who saw Ms Bruno in her rooms before the police arrived say that it would appear that her death was violent and her body was mutilated. Again, I have to stress that these are unconfirmed reports, but given the sheer quantity of police and forensic vans that are here I would suggest that it seems unlikely that her death was accidental or natural.'

'God.' Gwen's heart sank. Mutilated. It would be too much of a coincidence if this wasn't their alien.

'Are you saying this has something to do with you lot?' Beside her, Rhys's eyes were wide. 'Bloody hell, Gwen, but she's a star.'

Gwen shrugged. 'We all bleed, Rhys. We're all human.'

'Apart from maybe whatever killed her though, eh?' Rhys's voice was soft and Gwen didn't answer. There wasn't any need.

On screen, the newsreader touched her headset. 'I'm going to have to pause you there, Judy. We're just getting reports in that the body of a man has been discovered in the Angel Street park in Cardiff. The unidentified man was found by an early-morning dog walker in the area of the swings in the children's safe play area.' Gwen watched as she visibly flinched. 'The police have closed off the park and are treating the death as suspicious. Early reports suggest that the man had been violently mutilated.'

The repetition of the word made even the hardened journalist pause, and Gwen turned the TV off. She'd heard enough. Pulling her socks on, she stumbled into the hallway to grab her boots.

'I take it you're working late tonight?' Rhys leaned on the wall. She gave him a sad smile.

'Looks like it.'

There was a moment's silence while a thousand things went unsaid between them but were at the same time heard and understood.

Boots on, Gwen reached up and kissed him. 'I love you, Rhys Williams.'

'And I love you too, Gwen Cooper. And you bloody well take care out there.'

She grinned. 'I always do.' It was a lie that she knew he didn't believe but still liked to hear.

Seconds later, the door clicked shut, and Gwen Cooper belonged entirely to Torchwood again.

FOURTEEN

Stepping out of the lift that carried her down into the Hub, the first thing that hit Gwen was the sound of phones ringing. Given how few people were even aware of Torchwood's existence, that wasn't a good sign for the shape of the day ahead.

Not stopping to answer any, she found Ianto standing outside Jack's office. As always when he was frustrated with outside interference, their boss was pacing slightly behind his desk. From where Gwen was standing, it didn't look like Jack was getting much of a word in. She watched his lips.

'Yes, I understand… Yes sir, we're doing all we can…'

'Doesn't look good,' she muttered.

'First Minister for Wales was apparently a big fan.' Ianto didn't say who of. The answer was obvious. It wouldn't be the unnamed man in the park. 'As were several high-powered members of UNIT. We've had calls from both Manhattan and Geneva. They want to know if we've got a problem that we can't handle. Seems like everyone wants answers and fast.'

'What about the other body?'

'He's the same. Cutler's securing that scene now. Clothes and skin were fused as they were cut open. And just like Maria Bruno and the others, the vocal cords were gone.'

Gwen chewed the inside of her mouth. 'But no one would be causing all this fuss just for him or those three other poor sods, would they? How crap is that?'

Ianto shrugged. 'It's the way the world works.'

'Yeah, maybe, but it doesn't mean I have to like it. I want to get this bloody alien for all of them.' Biting her lip, Gwen tried to calm down. Snapping at Ianto was a tell-tale sign that she was getting emotionally involved in a case and, as much as she couldn't stop herself, she didn't want Ianto or Jack to see that it was getting to her.

'We all do, Gwen.' Ianto looked at her sideways. 'You think Jack is affected by celebrity? That he sees one victim as more important than another?'

Gwen stayed silent. Ianto was right. She couldn't blame him for the behaviour of the rest of the world. If anyone was untouched by its shallowness, then that person was Captain Jack Harkness. He'd seen too much. He was too different. Jack was, and she couldn't help but feel a tingle run down her spine, Jack was special.

On the other side of the glass, the subject of their conversation slammed down the receiver and flung open the door.

'Get those phones switched off. Now.' Striding past both Ianto and Gwen, Jack ran his hands through his hair. 'Jesus, I can't even hear myself think. If I have to say "yes sir" or "no sir" one more time today then I swear to God I think I'll shoot myself.'

Gwen glanced back at Jack's office and the old Second World War revolver that lay on his desk. 'So you think adding a headache to your problems will help us sort this mess out, then?'

Jack glared at her. 'Whereas you seem to think humour will?'

Her smile fell. Gwen could see that he was tired and his patience was wearing thin. While she'd been home with Rhys, he'd been here working.

'Sorry.'

He waved her apology away. 'Not your fault. Just too much bureaucracy for this time in the morning.' He took a deep breath and planted his hands on his hips.

Behind them, Ianto flicked a switch and the sound of telephones abruptly ceased. The Hub fell mercifully silent.

Jack finally smiled. 'Thank you.' He leaned against a workstation and let out a long sigh, his shoulders slumping slightly as they released some tension.

'Have you been working all night?' Gwen asked. Over by the coffee machine, Ianto set the water burbling.

'In the words of the great Lionel Richie, I have indeed been working all night long.' Jack looked up. 'But it was worth it.'

Both Ianto and Gwen stared.

'This isn't the time for a dramatic pause,' Gwen said finally. Her heart was thumping hard. 'What have you found?'

'I think I know who our alien is. Or at least where he comes from.'

Gwen looked over at Ianto and saw her own excitement reflected there. Five people were dead, and they hadn't been able to do anything about it. This was the first time they'd had anything that even resembled a lead.

Jack leaned over the large computer screen next to the Rift monitor. 'Come take a look.'

Ianto and Gwen leaned in on either side of him, and Gwen wondered if Ianto felt the same slight electric charge when his arm brushed against Jack's that she did. Probably. And probably a lot more. After all, their relationship was somewhat more intimate. For a moment her mind drifted, wondering not for the first time, how differently Jack would touch her from how he touched Ianto. Heat crept into her face and, frowning, she forced herself to focus on the screen. This *really* wasn't the time for that kind of daydream.

'What are we looking at?' she asked.

'This, my friends, is what the furthest corner of the known universe looks like.' Jack hesitated. 'Known to Earth, anyway.'

Beneath the gridlines marking out coordinates, the screen was filled with swirls of coloured gases and dark spots of various shapes that Gwen could only imagine were planets. Dotted more sporadically were brighter orbs. Suns.

'Isn't it amazing?' Jack's voice had taken on the hint of childish wonder and enthusiasm that Gwen had heard so much less of in recent months. It made her heart glow warm inside her. Her own sun. She looked over at the handsome man and he turned away from the screen for a second and grinned at her. Maybe he was their sun, she thought. And like the planets tugged in by gravity, once they'd been pulled into his orbit there was no real way out. Other than Retcon or death. And neither was a good option.

'So one of these planets is inhabited then?' Ianto asked. 'Which one?'

Jack laughed. 'Jeez, Ianto, all your years in Torchwood and that's the limit of your imagination?' He shook his head. 'There are thousands of planets on that screen, and hundreds of them are inhabited.' He grinned. 'And some of them are pretty good fun to visit.' He nudged the young man beside him. 'You'd love it. Beautiful boys, beautiful girls…' He paused, and shrugged. 'Well, near enough boys and girls. Humanoid at least.'

'Are we getting off the point here?' Standing back a little, Gwen folded her arms across her chest.

'Just giving you the full tour.' Jack's eyes narrowed. 'See here.' He pointed to the top left-hand corner of the flat monitor. This area of space was darker, the stars spread more infrequently and glowing less brightly as if fighting to stay burning against the blackness that threatened to swallow them up. Gwen could just about make out the occasional darker spot within the shadowy surrounds.

'Are those planets?' she asked, pointing one out.

'Uh-huh.' Jack nodded. 'And I think our alien comes from that one.'

He indicated a blur of darkness that was so far to the edge of the screen it was almost out of view.

'It doesn't look much like a planet,' Ianto said. 'Looks like a ball of gas.'

Gwen wasn't sure how Ianto could tell. Space was just space to her. It was only when it brought its business to Earth that she paid it any attention.

Jack stood up. 'That's because the planet itself is tiny, but it's wrapped in this black atmosphere. I'm not even sure it is gas. But whatever it is, it houses the inhabitants of the planet. They spend most of their time invisible in it, with no real form to speak of, each one simply a dark shadow lost in a cocoon of nothing wrapped around solid earth.' His voice was soft and serious. 'They choose to spend their lives disembodied and only re-form into their humanoid shapes in order to mate. It was thousands of years before anyone else in the galaxy even realised there was life on it.'

Ianto glanced at Jack. 'Well, we're looking for something that can change its shape and get through small spaces. I guess if one of these aliens were in its formless state that would fit the criteria. It would also explain some of the element of surprise. If it didn't take its solid shape until the last moment, there would be no time for the victim to call for help.'

'Exactly,' Jack said.

'They're not friendly then, on this planet?' Gwen asked. 'Although I suppose we can tell that from their habit of ripping out people's vocal cords.'

Jack shook his head. 'No, they're not friendly. But they're not unfriendly either.'

'How do you mean?'

'It's known as the Silent Planet. It doesn't have any other name because the creatures that live on it have no communication with the outside universe. They don't name themselves. Therefore they didn't name their planet.' He sighed. 'It's kind of a forgotten place. I'm surprised I even had it in the database. Must have been feeling thorough that day.'

'They don't have names?' Gwen looked at him. 'So how do they identify each other? Smell?'

Jack frowned and thrust his hands into his pockets thoughtfully. 'They *don't* identify each other. That's the point. It's known as the Silent Planet because there is no communication. They exist entirely contained within themselves from birth. There's no speech, no touch. Nothing. The idea of sharing their existence with another being is abhorrent to them.' His frown deepened. 'That's what the studies show at any rate. I mean, it's not as if you can just drop in and ask them. And even if you could then they wouldn't have a language to answer you with, so I'll take the researchers' word for it.'

'They never communicate with anyone at all?' For a moment Gwen tried to imagine how that would feel. The closest she could get was remembering a film she'd seen about a deaf, dumb and blind girl who'd eventually learned to read Braille and write. But even then she'd had touch. She had *known* other people. 'Must be lonely.'

'Guess it would seem that way to us. But it's the way they live. So to them it's perfectly natural. Our world would be a nightmare to them.'

The coffee machine gargled and spat the last of the boiling water through the filter and into the sizzling jug. Ianto was still staring at the screen as if the image would somehow force everything else to make sense, so Gwen went and poured, suddenly aware of every sound; the gentle thwump of her boots on the tiled floor underneath, the soft whisper of the milk hitting the base of the mugs, and then the clear tinkle of the metal spoon against ceramic as she stirred. They were noises that she almost didn't hear normally, they were just part of life. She tried to imagine silence – the non-existence of sound. She couldn't. Blowing her hair out of her face, she picked up the mugs and headed back. Ianto was still looking puzzled.

'So what happened? If our world would be such a nightmare to them, and I can see how it would be, then how did one of them end up here?'

Jack shrugged. 'What do we know about the Rift?

It brings stuff to Earth that doesn't belong here. And sometimes it takes people away to where they don't belong as well.' He sipped his coffee. 'Maybe the Rift has opened up on the Silent Planet, or near it, and pulled someone through.'

'It still doesn't make sense.' Gwen's brow furrowed. 'Imagine if you were suddenly taken from that planet to this one where everything is about sound and communication. TV, radio, constant traffic noise, mobile phones...' She stretched her hands out as if to elaborate her point. Even in that movement there was communication. 'It would send any creature insane.'

'Maybe it is insane,' Ianto cut in. 'Maybe that's why it's killing people.'

Gwen shook her head. 'No, these deaths are too organised. If this creature was insane, it would just be charging through the streets of Cardiff ripping apart everyone it came across. This alien is selecting its victims specifically.'

'Singers.'

'Good singers,' added Jack. He looked over to Gwen. 'I think you're right. I'm not convinced that this alien is crazy. What it's doing might be crazy, but I don't think the essence of the alien is. Hell, I don't think it would even understand the concept.'

'Maybe the Rift didn't drag it through. Maybe it came through because it wanted to.' Ianto's eyes were back on the small dark corner of the screen that showed a place so very, very – *impossibly* – far away.

'It's a possibility,' said Jack. 'But one that we may never find the answer to, even if we do manage to catch this thing.'

Gwen looked up. 'And do we have a plan for doing that?'

'Ah…' Jack sighed and looked at his expectant team. 'Knowing what it is doesn't give us any help in finding it. The Rift activity only spikes pretty much immediately before an attack, which makes me think that this creature is somehow hiding just inside the Rift and only coming through when it's ready to kill.'

Gwen stared at Jack, and then glanced over at Ianto, whose face looked as surprised as she felt. 'Hiding *inside* the Rift? Is that even possible?'

Jack matched her gaze. 'You know as well as I do, with the Rift, anything could be possible.'

'So we're in exactly the same position we were in yesterday?' Ianto asked.

'No. We now know we *can* catch it. A portable prison cell will work on it, at least for an hour.'

'And then what will we do with it?' Gwen peered over the top of her coffee mug. 'Sing it a lullaby and send it back through the Rift?'

'Let's worry about that when we've caught it.'

'Which brings us back to the original question.' Ianto finally looked away from the screen and back at Jack. 'How are we going to do that?'

Jack's sparkling grin flashed. 'We're going to have to set a trap.' The sound of his mobile ringing pealed out from Jack's pocket and he groaned. 'Great.' Pushing away from the workstation, he took his coffee with him and headed back to his office. 'Gwen, I want you to get hold of Cutler and bring him in on this one. If we set a trap, I want it done with him in the know.'

'Are you sure?'

'Yeah.' Jack paused at his door and looked back over his shoulder. 'I read his file last night. I figure maybe Torchwood owes him.' The phone refused to go silent. 'Ianto, you get all the information from the crime scenes and see if there's anything we can use. Anything at all. Let's not lose any more people to this thing.'

Closing the door, he finally flipped open his phone. Gwen sighed and pulled out her own mobile to find out exactly where Cutler was. Up to his eyes in crap, she should imagine, just like Jack Harkness was.

FIFTEEN

Journalists swarmed outside the police station like summer flies on roadkill and, pushing through them to reach the stairs, Gwen fought the urge to swat them away. What did they really want here: answers, or news of another gory death? Cardiff was selling record numbers of newspapers today and these vampires weren't going to want that to stop. Not just yet anyway.

She bit back her disgust. Journalists were the leaders in the 'bad things happen to other people' brigade, as if their own lives were wipe-clean. One day, they'd each find out different. If they happened to become the news rather than just scavenging for it.

'Are you with the police, lady?'

A young man followed her up the stairs and tugged her sleeve slightly too insistently, making the collar of her jacket cut into her neck. 'You got any news on the Bruno murder? What about these other killings? They all by the same guy?'

Yanking her arm free, Gwen glared at him. 'I've just lost my cat, that's all. Now get off me.'

Taking the last few stairs two at a time, she pushed through the heavy door, shoving past the constable who was guarding the entrance, and headed straight for the desk sergeant.

'Gwen Cooper. Torchwood.' The man behind the desk was a stranger to her. He raised his greying head and looked her up and down, and the disgruntled look was clear on his middle-aged face. She couldn't blame him entirely. The police knew very little about Torchwood, other than that they turned up and took over every now and again, and that could get under the skin. Still, they were all just doing their jobs, and ultimately they were all on the same side, even if it didn't always feel like it.

Staring him down, she didn't smile. She was long past the stage of feeling split loyalties between her old job and her new work. Gwen was Torchwood through and through.

'Where's DI Cutler? He's expecting me.'

The sergeant stared at her for a moment before picking up the phone. 'I've got a Gwen Cooper here for DI Cutler.' He glanced up at her again, his disdain obvious. 'Apparently he's expecting her. Says she's Torchwood.'

Gwen kept her own expression neutral. She knew his type; they were in all walks of life. The kind of man that was never going to respect a woman under 35, someone who was always going to think she had got to wherever she was by shagging someone.

He put the phone down, and nodded very slightly towards the double doors. 'You'll find him through there somewhere. The incident room's on the second floor, but he might be out the back having a smoke.' He smiled. 'But you're Torchwood. You should find him no problem.'

Gwen smiled back. 'I know where the incident room is.' Despite her smile, the words had an unmistakable acid edge. 'I used to work here. But thank you for being so helpful.'

Leaving the sergeant to stew into his tea, she strode into the heart of the station. Phones rang, and printers rattled off reports and incident logs. She could feel the heightened energy in the air. While the rest of Cardiff was focused on the murders, there were men and women housed in this building who had to get on with solving all the other crimes that were still insisting on being committed daily: the domestic violence, the car thefts, the vandalisms. It was never ending.

'Hi.' A smart WPC was scurrying by, a pile of papers in her hands, and Gwen stopped her with a gentle touch on the arm. She'd been just like that in these very corridors not so very long ago. 'I'm looking for DI Cutler. The miserable bastard on the desk said he might be out the back having a fag?'

The young woman flashed a quick smile. 'Oh yes. He is. I saw him heading out five minutes ago. Just follow the corridor round and right at the end there's a fire escape. He's normally there.' Her smile lingered a little and, thanking her, Gwen wondered if the WPC had considered taking up smoking just to get to share that fire escape with the untidy London detective. Gwen wouldn't blame her. If she was single herself, she'd be tempted. There was something about a damaged man with a chip on his shoulder that was too bloody attractive. And she might not know Cutler well, but she knew him well enough to know that he fulfilled both those criteria.

The fire door was ajar and, pushing it open, she found Cutler leaning on the railings and staring into the alleyway. Steam chugged out of vents on the wall opposite, which, if Gwen had her mental geography right, was the back of Giovanni's Trattoria. She suddenly wondered if this street even had a name, housing, as it did, only the ugly backsides of offices and businesses.

Taking a long drag on his cigarette, Cutler didn't even turn round. 'I was hoping you wouldn't find me out here, Scully.'

Stepping forward, Gwen joined him, peering out into the unsightly street full of bins and potholes now filled with dirty rain water. At least that had stopped for a while, even if the clouds were darkly ominous above them. 'We're Torchwood. We can find you anywhere.'

'Really?' Cutler didn't contain his sarcasm. 'Then maybe rather than finding me, you should go find the bad guy.'

'Fair comment.' She paused. 'I saw the reporters out

the front. I take it you're not having the best day.'

For the first time, Cutler turned to look at her, his haunted eyes both defensive and appraising. 'The hyenas I can handle. Trust me, I've dealt with worse.' He paused and sucked on his cigarette again before flicking it out onto the tarmac below. 'Although if this isn't sorted soon they'll be dragging all that shit up again. That'll be fun.'

Gwen noticed a flash of gold on his left hand and took a second to realise it was a ring. He was married. The information jarred in her head. That couldn't be right. He was too disaffected, too distant from the world to have anything like what she and Rhys shared. He was widowed or divorced. Had to be. Curiosity aroused, Gwen wished she'd taken a peek at his file. Maybe she'd get a look at it later.

'Today I've been doing what I do worst,' Cutler continued, peering thoughtfully into his cigarette packet. 'Facing grieving people and having to lie and tell them that I'm chasing leads and going to catch whoever's doing this. Like I'm bloody Morse or Taggart or some other fictional character who never fails to help good win over evil.' He paused. 'What a pile of shit this is.'

Feeling his tension escaping with his words, Gwen stayed silent. He needed to vent his frustration and it might as well be at her. An extra ten minutes or so wasn't going to make any difference. More steam pumped out from the restaurant opposite, drifting towards them before dying somewhere in the middle of the alley, ripped apart by the cool air.

'Bruno's husband's a broken man.' Cutler tucked the cigarettes back in his pocket but stayed where he was. 'But then I think he was pretty much there before this happened. He's got that look of a man on the edge of collapse. She was going to fire him, he said. Sack him and divorce him.' He raised an eyebrow. 'She definitely would have done when she found out that he owed the tax man a bloody fortune. I don't even think it's his fault. From what I gather, she liked to live like a star and her best days were behind her.'

Gwen lifted her chin to let the cool breeze touch her face. 'Poor workman blames his tools.'

Cutler laughed a little; a soft, hollow sound. 'Yeah, and he definitely is her tool. Still,' he went on, 'Martin Meloy says he didn't care about that. He reckons he loved her.' He shook his head slightly. 'And I believe the sad little twat.' He pulled the cigarettes back out of his pocket and defiantly lit one. 'Love. Who'd bother? It only lets you down in the end.'

'Worth it sometimes, though.' Gwen looked down at her own wedding band.

Cutler laughed again. 'Give it time and some challenges. Then come back and tell me you're still happy.' At least this time there was a twinkle of genuine humour in his eyes, and for a brief moment Gwen saw almost behind the dark shadows in them to the person he might once have been.

He frowned. 'Anyway. Where's Mulder?'

Gwen smiled. 'Captain Jack Harkness is spending the

morning doing what he does worst. He's strapped to his desk, fielding calls he doesn't want to take.'

'Him too? Maybe we've got more in common than I gave him credit for. So, what's he sent you to tell me?' He raised an eyebrow. 'Does he want to make sure the puppet doesn't try pulling his own strings?'

The bitter edge stung through the last sentence, and Gwen felt her own hackles rising a little. 'I don't know what happened with you and Torchwood One, that's not my business, but you really don't know Jack Harkness if you think that's how he sees or treats people.' She paused. 'He wants to set some kind of trap for the alien and he wants you in on it.' The first drops of rain fell heavily from the over-burdened sky. 'He thinks Torchwood owes you.'

They stared at each other for a long moment, and then Cutler shrugged. 'Mulder may be right on that one.'

The fire door opened and the constable who had been keeping an eye on the journalists at the main entrance to the station peered round the door.

'Sorry to disturb you, sir.' He looked warily over at Gwen before continuing. 'There's a bloke at the front desk. Says he wants to see you.'

Cutler snorted. 'Tell him to join the queue.'

'I did tell him you were in a meeting, but he's refusing to leave. I think he's a bit hysterical. Says he's that poof's boyfriend. Says you spoke to him this morning.'

'That *poof*'s name was Ben Pritchard,' Cutler growled, making the young constable visibly flinch and pull back slightly behind the safety of the heavy door. 'And as we're as yet unable to tell his boyfriend who was responsible for ripping his loved one apart in a park, I suggest you start showing a little more respect.'

The constable's face was beetroot. 'Sorry, sir. Didn't mean anything by it.'

'And that,' Cutler dropped the half-smoked cigarette and left it to die on the damp ground before letting his eyes slash through the man as they passed him, 'makes it worse.'

Drew Powell was sitting dejectedly on the hard bench that lined one bleak wall of the reception area, his face blotchy from tears, his fingers worrying at a cotton handkerchief. Gwen looked at the chubby man. His short hair was fluffy and unkempt where she thought it would normally be carefully styled with wax or gel and his eyes were exhausted.

'I told you to pack up and go home, Mr Powell.' Cutler's voice was weary, but kind, as if he felt some of the other man's grief personally. 'We'll let you know when we can release the body. Go back to your family and friends. This place can't be any good for you.'

Drew Powell stood up and paced. 'I can't go home. Not now.' He paused and looked from Cutler to Gwen and back again. 'I saw the news. Couldn't help it. Maria Bruno's dead too. You didn't tell me.' He held the handkerchief up to his nose, pressing it against his face, sucking the smell in rather than using it to clean himself. It wasn't his, Gwen realised. It was Ben's. Powell was using it like a comfort blanket.

'Do you think whoever killed her killed my Ben too? They said… they said she was mutilated. Just like Ben.' His voice dropped to barely a whisper, his energy draining.

Cutler glanced at Gwen and shrugged slightly. 'I can't discuss the details of the case with you. Not at this stage. It could jeopardise the ongoing investigation. I'm sorry.' His apology sounded hollow.

Drew turned his desperate stare on Gwen. 'You can't tell me anything?'

'Detective Inspector Cutler's right,' she told him. 'I know this is terrible, but the best thing for you is to go home and grieve. We'll do everything we can.'

The chubby man lifted his chin and took a deep, snotty breath through his nose. He pursed his lips. 'I am not going to be going home. I shall sing in that competition.' His lips wobbled a little as tears threatened, but he swallowed them back. 'Pritchard and Powell came second last year, and we would have won this year. I'm not letting Ben down now. I'll sing on my bloody own if I have to!'

Drew turned on one heel in a dramatic pre-*exit stage left* moment worthy of any theatre in the world, but it only seemed pathetically fragile in this situation. He was about to flounce out of the station and into the glare of the hungry media, when Gwen felt the tingle of an idea run through her. Reaching forward, she touched his arm. He turned.

'What?'

Although they were the only people in the front of the station apart from the desk sergeant, she stepped in closer. Beside her, Cutler did the same.

'What are you doing, Scully?'

She didn't look at him, focusing on Drew. 'What if we could find you another singing partner?'

He stared, his pale eyes searching into hers. 'I don't want to sing with anyone else.'

'But what if you could sing with someone and maybe have a chance of helping catch whoever did this to Ben?'

'Scully—'

She glared at Cutler cutting him dead. 'The name's Gwen Cooper. And back off.'

Drew's eyes widened. 'I'll do it,' he whispered.

'It's too dangerous,' Cutler snapped. He looked at the small, chubby man, whose eyes at last held something other than sheer desolation. 'I'm sorry. It's too risky.'

'But it's my risk, isn't it?' Drew stood up close to Cutler and pulled himself as tall as he could manage. 'And Ben wouldn't hesitate... wouldn't have hesitated... to do it for me.'

Gwen was pleased to hear that the smaller man had his own reserve of steel to coat his words with.

She pressed speed dial on her mobile. 'Ianto. Tell Jack I think I've got a plan.' She paused. 'And it involves you.'

SIXTEEN

Be careful what you wish for… The old saying ran through Ianto's head as he walked up the stone-flagged stairs to the tiny Gothic chapel of St Jude's. Its dark walls were aged and weather-beaten and, surrounded as it was by the comparatively vast and bright office buildings that had grown up in the nearby streets since the 1970s, it was almost forgotten and invisible, just a dark shadow of history clinging to existence against the inevitability of change.

Pulling open the heavy door, he stepped into the vestry, immediately shivering in the warmth. The bricks and mortar may have been ancient, but the inside was relatively modern and well maintained. There were no draughts or bad lighting and the pews were light wood, covered in soft, fresh, red bench cushions.

Walking up the aisle, the words echoed again in his head. *Be careful what you wish for. It may come true.* He was definitely learning the meaning of that. Yes, he'd been stuck in the Hub a bit too much recently, but this plan of Gwen's wasn't exactly what he'd meant by wanting to get out more. Chasing down Weevils, yes. Tracking alien technology on the move, yes. Being stuck with Drew Powell all bloody day, no. That had definitely not been what he'd wanted. It wasn't as if it gave them any more than an outside chance of catching the damned thing.

He took a sip from his strong takeaway coffee and then tore open the wrapper of a chocolate bar with his teeth. He was going to need the energy. Mentally and emotionally at any rate. The chocolate and caramel tasted good, and the next sip of coffee melted the remains in his mouth, making sure none escaped the trip into his blood stream. The coffee was over-brewed, but at least the taste of chocolate overpowered it slightly. He needed it, however bad it tasted. There couldn't be enough sugar and caffeine to help him cope with Drew Powell. The man strained even Ianto Jones's natural calm reserve. As far as Ianto was concerned, Ben Pritchard must have been a saint.

Putting the coffee cup down, Ianto touched the Bluetooth device attached to his ear. 'Break's over. I'm back in location.'

'Good. We're in place.' Jack's voice was clear in his head. 'Hope Cardiff's finest male voice choir are ready to make some more beautiful music together.'

'Ha, bloody ha.' Ianto ended the connection and waited for Drew, suddenly feeling very alone in the sanctity of the church, even though Jack and Gwen were in the SUV, only fifty metres away at the most, hidden up a side street away from the glare of overhead lighting. They were parked on a double yellow, but Cutler had wryly commented that parking tickets were one thing he *could* take care of.

At least there hadn't been any fresh killings, which was a good thing. It was always possible, if not likely, that the alien had been taken back through the Rift and was long gone. It seemed more probable, however, that there had been a lot less rehearsing going on in the city after the death of Maria Bruno. Many of the competitors had simply packed their bags and quit. Five of their number had been murdered, and their logic seemed to be that if the killer could get to someone as famous as Maria Bruno, then no one was safe. Those with weaker stomachs and lesser talents had vanished, and those who were determined to stick it out and see the competition through were reluctant to give the songs full voice. Yet still Ianto and Drew belting their numbers out all day wasn't bringing the alien to them.

They had picked St Jude's because it was secluded and as close to the epicentre of the deaths as they could find. Cutler had used his team to call every hired space in Cardiff to find out when they were booked out and when they were empty. Ianto and Drew had been rehearsing all day, and would keep on into the night if they had to.

Police cars were stationed throughout the city during peak rehearsal times, each with instructions to contact Cutler immediately should they see anything unusual or suspicious. But Ianto reckoned that, given that the city was pretty much in mourning, he and Drew were the only ones singing with any vigour in its streets.

Drew's voice carried out from the small room to the left of the altar, rising up and down the notes of the octaves, and Ianto jumped slightly, before smiling at his own nerves and then sipping more foul coffee, which probably wasn't helping the general undertone of tension that filled his veins. So he wasn't alone after all. Still, he'd give himself a couple more minutes before letting the other man know he was back.

Unusual or suspicious. Or perhaps a shape-changing alien that likes to rip people open and demolecularise their vocal cords. That would be more precise.

If it had been up to Jack or Cutler, the competition would have been cancelled completely, but that idea had been squashed from on high. The competition was good for Wales. It was a celebration of everything that was finest about the small nation. It was good for tourism. And, of course, this year it was being *televised*. Whoever it was that had been on the phone to Jack had definitely laboured that point. Ianto had heard every word, and he'd been standing several metres away. The competition finals were to go ahead. And it was up to Torchwood to make sure they did so smoothly and safely. Ianto could understand their concerns. Seeing a person ripped apart on stage during a live television show probably wouldn't go down well with the viewing public. Especially before the watershed.

And so here he was, hoping they could lure the alien. It was a one in a thousand shot, and so far there wasn't a glimmer of a spike in Rift activity. Ianto now had almost as little faith in the plan as he had faith in his own ability to sing.

Taking his damp jacket off, he dropped it onto one of the pews at the front and then put his coffee on top of the grand piano over to the right. Inside his trouser pocket the circular portable prison device felt heavy and awkward against his leg and served to remind him of exactly what he and Drew were really doing here.

It might not have been the kind of field work he'd hoped for, but it was still dangerous. Both he and Drew were taking risks with their lives, and as much as Ianto had got used to that concept during his years in Torchwood, it still came as a shock when the risks were for real. For Drew Powell, who was just an office-bound insurance broker, it must be frightening, especially on top of his loss.

'Drew?' Ianto called, feeling slightly bad about the irritation he felt. 'I'm out here.'

He shoved the final pieces of chocolate bar into his mouth and was washing it down with coffee when the chubby man bustled in from the antechamber.

He stared at Ianto, before one finger rose and pointed with venom towards the plastic coffee cup. 'I sincerely hope that is a black coffee.'

'It's a latte. Sorry, I should have brought you one. Didn't think.' Ianto held the cup forward. 'You can have some of mine if you like. Although I warn you, it's not the best. Didn't you go out and grab anything?'

Drew ignored the question, his chin wobbling as he glared. 'You're drinking a milky coffee before singing?' His eyes widened as they caught the crumpled chocolate bar wrapper unfurling on the piano top. '*And eating chocolate?*' His voice squeaked out from some reedy place at the top of his range, and Ianto's irritation flushed back into his cheeks.

'Is that a problem? I was hungry.' *I've been bloody working all day,* he wanted to add, but he bit the words back in a gulp.

Drew snatched at the wrapper and the cup, flamboyantly tossing them into the waste-paper basket tucked behind the piano, leaving a trail of creamy coffee splattered up the back wall that was not going to impress the vicar.

'Of course it's a problem,' he snapped, fingers fluttering through the empty air between them. 'You said you were a singer. Any singer worth his salt knows no red wine, chocolate or coffee before singing. It's death to the vocal cords.'

Half-listening, already resigned to disappointing his partner, Ianto thought Powell was lucky he wasn't aware of the irony of his words. They hadn't shared with him the nature of the mutilation his boyfriend had suffered. There was only so much that Drew Powell needed to

146

know, and that information was limited to knowing that they were trying to trap a serial killer.

'I'm sorry,' he muttered, feeling sorry for a lot of things, drinking coffee not amongst them.

Drew's hands gripped his comfortable hips and he shook his head. 'No wonder you're having problems getting a decent note out. Still, never mind. I'll have to work with what I've been given. Although what Ben would have made of it, I dread to think.' Hovering his finger over the play button on the portable stereo, Drew raised an eyebrow. 'Now, what do we have to remember?'

Ianto gritted his teeth against the patronising *'we'* and took a deep breath. 'Not to breathe with my shoulders and to tuck my diaphragm in.'

'Bravissimo.'

As the first strains of music started, Ianto wondered whether his love for the duet from *The Pearl Fishers* was lost for ever. It was beginning to feel like it might be.

The approaching dusk crept slowly across Cardiff, evening greedily consuming any light in the damp cool air and replacing it with an infectious grey gloom.

The streets were hushed, and even the traffic was moving with more caution, as if fearful that the mysterious killer that plagued the streets would follow the thrum of the engines and claim their drivers' lives and insides when they reached their destinations. Pedestrians peered cautiously over their shoulders and shivered at the headlines written boldly on A-boards, all declaring

No leads in hunt for Serial Slasher! City in terror! and found they huddled closer together as they scurried home.

Strange things often happened in Cardiff, and on a subconscious level its residents were toughened against them, but this was different. In the rain and the mist that poured in across the water, as if even the Bay itself could feel the anxiety that pulsed through the city's inhabitants, the fear that ate at the heart of the Welsh nation was like that which had haunted Whitechapel over a hundred years before. *Ripper. Slasher.* The words were too similar for most people's liking, and as more vivid details of the gruesome nature of the murders emerged, splattered across the pages of the papers, more residents hurried home to turn their lights on, lock the doors, and take comfort in each other's heat on their sofas.

In the pubs and bars, people watched each other carefully. Who could you trust? Really? Eyes were furtive, glancing up, down and around. Danger could lurk in any direction. There were whispers of heavy feet on roofs, strange figures seen loitering in dark places, there and then not there. Wild stories bred by feverish imaginations.

Cars headed out, away from the bright lights of the Bay, many visitors cutting short their trips, declaring to disappointed hoteliers and bed and breakfast owners that 'the weather was too unpleasant', but the delicate tremble in the hands that signed bills and receipts hinted at the truth. Until the police could catch this killer, then someone had to be next. And no one wanted it to be them. But they all waited in anticipation of the next set of grisly details. There was nothing like a murder to make you feel alive, after all.

SEVENTEEN

Adrienne Scott chucked her robe and wig onto her desk next to all the case files that were screaming for her attention, and shut the door to her office in chambers behind her. Her head was thumping, and all she wanted to do was go and drink a large glass of white wine. It had been one of those days, and tomorrow she had to visit with Ryan before going straight into court so that one wasn't going to be any better. She avoided contemplating the tragedy that a bottle of wine seemed like the only occasional respite from her life.

Leaving her overcoat undone, she let the light drizzle land on her face and clothes. It was refreshing and let her brain breathe. It might even help shift this headache before painkillers were needed. She glanced at her watch. Quarter to five. It was almost a respectable time for the first drink of the evening, and she'd at least arranged to meet a friend so that she could kid herself the wine was part of a social occasion rather than the social occasion being there to support the wine.

Her heels tapped across the small square as she stretched out the no-nonsense stride that had, many times over, warned any potential suitors away before they'd even approached her to speak. I can cope, her walk said. I don't need you to complicate my life. It's complicated enough. Now sod off, before we start to like each other.

Over on a corner, a choir of eight or ten bedraggled men and women were singing into the night air. *Don't let fear kill Cardiff's music!* proclaimed the banner they were holding over their heads, but they didn't seem to be singing with too much enthusiasm, apart from one woman at the front who was belting it out, a beatific smile plastered across her wet face. Her sharp barrister's eyes giving the singers a quick onceover, Adrienne decided it was probably this woman who was responsible for dragging the rest of them out into the cold streets. She had the look of a bossy cow.

There was no collection box at their feet, and Adrienne didn't smile as she passed. Music was one thing she could do without. Ryan had destroyed any enjoyment she'd ever got from singing. Glaring at the billboard posters still carrying the smiling face of the murdered opera singer, Adrienne thought she couldn't wait for the bloody competition to be over.

But, before that, she couldn't wait for that first glass of deliciously numbing Chardonnay.

Ianto's face was flushed as they reached the end of the piece. As much as he hated admitting it, Drew's advice was improving his voice. He was sounding almost half-decent now.

Drew clapped his hands together. 'Much better! Much better!' He paused. 'I mean you still occasionally have the tonal quality of a complete amateur, but on the whole your breathing is almost there.' He paced a little, shaking his shoulders out. 'The middle section is your weak point. You need to be *mezzo cantabile* and *mezzo diminuendo* in order for your *crescendo* to be more powerful.'

More slowly and more gently. Ianto seemed to be learning as much about Italian from Drew as he was about singing. That morning he'd suggested that it might be easier if Drew would just tell him what he meant in English. Drew hadn't even commented but said all he needed to about that with a disgusted glare.

The chubby man looked at him, his eyes narrowing. 'Yes, the breathing's there, and you're hitting most of the notes OK, but you're lacking feeling and without that the music's nothing.'

'What?' So much for feeling better about himself.

'Emotion!' Drew flung his arms above his head in a typically overdramatic gesture. 'This song is all about love and passion! Two men realising they've both fallen in love with the same illusion of a fantasy woman, and

153

then swearing their undying friendship despite this overwhelming passion they both feel.'

'I know what the bloody song's about,' Ianto sighed. 'That's my best. I can't do better.'

Drew shook his head. 'Yes, you can. I'm not talking about the notes, I'm talking about your expression.'

'I don't do expression. I keep my feelings to myself.'

'Doesn't take a genius to figure that out, darling.' Pressing the button to take the track back to the beginning, Drew shooed him backward. 'Just listen to me. I'll sing my part all the way through. Stand back and listen. You'll see what I mean.'

Ianto took a couple of steps backwards into the aisle. Folding his arms, he waited for the intro to finish and Drew to start. Watching the little man in front of him, he almost felt the change, as if the air trembled when he began to sing. Drew was no more than a few bars in when the hairs on the backs of Ianto's arms began to stand on end. His mouth dried as he let the music run through him, all the power of the melody and lyrics streaming out from Drew.

Ianto didn't feel his mouth open, and Drew definitely couldn't see how impressed his apprentice was because his own eyes were closed, his knees bending and body swaying as he set the song free to fill the church with its message of love more effectively than any sermon could.

Suddenly Ianto felt an ache inside, wishing he could have heard Ben Pritchard singing alongside his lover rather than his own wooden baritone. Even from a few metres away, he could make out the tears that ran occasionally down Drew's face, as if, for the first time since Ben's terrible death, he was truly letting his grief out, singing it out to the world. It was beautiful.

Jack drummed his fingers on the steering wheel inside the SUV. Sitting around doing nothing was not something he did well. Even with an apparently endless life ahead of him, it was a frustrating waste of time. Behind him, DI Cutler beat out a similar quiet rhythm on the back of the leather seat. It seemed the policeman wasn't too hot on inactivity either. No one spoke. They'd long ago run out of conversation, and the tension of the alien's no-show hummed throughout the car.

Gritting his teeth, Jack stared out into the gloom of the falling night. Where the hell had the creature from the Silent Planet gone? It had to be out there somewhere and why the hell had it stopped attacking after such a frenzied start? And who the hell knew where it was really from anyway? All he had was guesswork and probability.

As the hours ticked past, he had found he was starting to doubt himself, and self-doubt was another thing Captain Jack Harkness didn't do well. It irritated him. But this case had the taste of unfinished business, and that he couldn't doubt. The feeling came from his gut and that was rarely wrong. There was a chance he might mess up the small details, but never the big picture. He'd seen too much not to trust his instincts. Maybe the alien was lying low for a while. Maybe they'd have to sit around waiting until they'd all gone crazy, or Ianto was taking to the stage of the Millennium Centre, or next year's competition came round, but it would be back. Jack just knew.

Beside him Gwen bristled, and Jack knew what she was going to say before her mouth opened. His pulse quickened.

'Rift activity.'

'Where?' The drumming of fingers stopped.

'Everywhere.' Gwen frowned at the screen. 'Tiny spikes. Nothing major. I don't understand. They seem to be all over the city.'

'That's not helping, Gwen.' Jack gripped the car door handle. They couldn't screw this up.

'I'm just telling you what the machine is telling me.'

'Don't just read it. *Predict* where it's going.'

Gwen flashed her dark, angry eyes at him. 'I'm not bloody Tosh. I'm doing my…' Her gaze back on the screen, she tilted her head. 'Hang on. They're converging. This is weird. It's like they're pulling together or something.' Recoiling, she flinched. 'Shit! We've got a big spike.' She looked up. 'It's coming together here! At the church!'

Jack was out of the SUV before she'd finished her sentence, arms pumping as he sprinted up through the alley, Cutler's heavier tread echoing his own a few paces behind. The church grew up from the corner and he pushed himself towards it.

EIGHTEEN

Drew was just reaching the peak of his piece when Ianto's muscles stiffened slightly, his primal senses aware of danger even before it had quite arrived. Lost in the music, Drew sang on, but Ianto was no longer absorbed in his talent, the sound now merely a distraction as he glanced around trying to home in on what had disturbed him. He shivered, a chill running down his spine. Something was wrong.

He looked up, just before a window set high in the wall above him smashed, sending shards of crimson-coloured glass plummeting to the floor like bloodied hail and carrying within it a figure that disintegrated into nothing as he tried to focus on it, becoming only a substance hidden between the fragments. Ducking instinctively, Ianto yanked the portable device free and, crouching, peered upwards. Where the hell was it?

Drew had stopped singing and the backing music continued plaintively as the chubby man stared desperately at Ianto, fear wreaking havoc in his eyes before something caught at his chest and, as he gasped, his gaze dragged reluctantly to his left. Staying low and hidden by the aisle, Ianto moved forward, looking to see what Drew was staring at with such unconfined horror.

A dark void of blackness that was smeared against the wall of the church began to re-form, shaping itself into something solid. Watching the moulding of limbs and torso completing, cold gripped Ianto's chest and it took all his effort to touch his earpiece.

'Jack.' The name was suddenly unfamiliar, and for a moment Ianto couldn't see Jack's face in the space in his brain where it belonged.

'It's here.' The words rasped out of him, no purity in the sound and no breathing from his diaphragm, just sheer effort and desperation, and the minute he'd spoken he wasn't sure he could repeat the sentence, even if his life depended on it.

Life.

He dragged his head upwards against the weight of emptiness that was pressing his soul into isolation. *Drew's life.* The chubby man was just a few metres away, gazing, his mouth drooping open as if he'd forgotten how to close it. Ianto didn't look over at the alien. He couldn't. If he did, he was afraid he'd never move from the spot again.

Keeping his eyes down, he rushed towards the frozen Drew, needing to come between him and the creature. In the corner of his eye there was a sudden movement and, twisting his head, he saw the strange metallic man, his solid body a network of sharp fractures. Caught in that frozen moment as they both leapt towards Drew, Ianto thought the black silent void of its home planet leaked through those cracks, infecting the air around it with sheer emotional desolation, as if there was too much for the one creature to house.

Ianto wanted to weep, but had forgotten how. His own action was clumsily human, slow and heavy, but the alien moved fast and jerkily like the flickering image of a broken film; in one spot at one moment, and beside Drew in the next, its attention focused only on the chubby man as if the Torchwood operative didn't even exist.

Shrieking like a savage, Ianto threw himself at it, his finger on the button of the portable prison. The power of his cry deadened in the air around the alien and, taking a deep breath, Ianto's hand grabbed the creature's arm. His shriek died with the contact and what it brought with it. Coldness shocked its way throughout his own system and an instant silence emptied his mind. The world was empty. The world was dead. With the last drip of thought, he squeezed his numb finger down.

The alien tossed him aside as if he were no more than an irritating gnat, hurling him sideways and into the piano. His head slamming hard into the sharp edge of the wood, Ianto watched in despair as the portable prison tumbled to the back of the church, activated, but with nothing in its field but empty air. Blood trickled into his eye, and he was glad of its warmth. Black pain throbbed through his head and, just as unconsciousness gripped him, he heard Drew Powell begin to scream.

Jack pushed through the double doors from the vestry, not pausing in his stride as his eyes took in the scene ahead. Broken glass littered the pews, crunching underneath his boots. Beyond the altar and the piano, the blue light of the prison cylinder shone upwards but it was empty; Jack didn't even have to look at it to know that.

Drew Powell lay on the floor, the alien crouching over him. Its head was tossed back in an awful mockery of a howl, the pit of its mouth stretched open in a silent scream, pouring black emptiness out into the church. Its arm stretched out towards Powell's neck, the limb dissolved towards the end, the hand nothing more than a black streak that cut into the singer's neck like a scalpel.

'No!' Pulling his gun free from its holster, Jack fired into the alien's back before running forward. Drew Powell was not going to die. Not when they were this close, God dammit. Recoiling from the bullet, the creature twisted round, its rage and disappointment glaring out at Jack from two blazes of red in the pits of its dark eyes. In a split second it was on its feet, the shot seeming to have caused no lasting damage.

Jack's lungs burned with cold as he stretched out to grab it, but he was an instant too slow, its body dissolving into blackness as the shadow pulled away and upwards, escaping through the broken window high on the wall, leaving Jack with only the slightest damp taste of its presence. Panting, he filled the space the alien had vacated, and black rage filled him.

'Shit!' Behind him, Cutler turned back. 'I'll go after it!'

'No point. Call an ambulance.' Falling to his knees, Jack looked down into the gurgling mess of Drew's neck. A slice ran down from his chin to his Adam's apple, sticky blood pumping slowly out. The cut was bad, and God only knew how deep it went, but Jack knew that if an artery had been severed they'd all be covered. Maybe there was a chance. Cursing under his breath, he chewed on his own frustration and anger. There had to be a goddamn chance. Gently, he lifted the man up slightly so he could breathe without drowning in his own blood, and stroked his forehead.

'It's OK. You're going to be OK.' Watching the beads of damp sweat forming on the shivering man's ashen face, he hoped he wasn't lying. 'You hang in there, you hear me? Help's on its way.' Somewhere in the distance, giving his words weight, a siren began to wail through the night.

Behind him, Ianto groaned.

'Gwen!' Jack called over his shoulder. 'Is Ianto all right?'

'He's got a nasty cut. But I think he'll live.'

There was a long pause.

'What are we going to do now, Jack?' Her voice was

161

soft and low and, feeling the warm blood of the injured man coating his hands, Jack was glad he didn't have to look at her face when he answered.

'I don't know, Gwen. I just don't know.'

NINETEEN

The hospital was alive with sound from the moment they arrived.

It seemed to Gwen that each area of the building had its own unique orchestra to identify it. When she'd visited the witnesses to Richard Greenwood's death, there had been only the hum of lights and the calm whispering of shoes and skirts as they had travelled through the ward like ghosts, pausing to smile and check temperatures and tick lists on charts. Patients had been reading books and magazines and occasionally chatting quietly to visitors as they discussed what they might do when they were released. Much of the time had been filled with the slow breathing of sleep as fractured bones and damaged organs mended. Peace and quiet had reigned in a place where recovery was almost a certainty, and days were marked off with the delivery of meals and afternoon naps after some daytime TV.

This time, as she leapt out of the ambulance and ran into the hospital behind the paramedics, Gwen would have known she was in the Accident and Emergency department even if she had been blinded. Noise danced and partied in the bright corridors, whooping with glee at every new arrival. The wheels of the trolley carrying Drew Powell squealed and rattled as they pushed forwards, crashing through doors as nurses and doctors called out to each other for drips, and numbers and pressures in a language of their own that just created dread in those excluded from its understanding. Behind hastily drawn curtains, the burned and the broken and the drunk ranted and raved, screaming and sobbing for help or a loved one, either in pain or in panic. Nurses' feet thumped hard against the floor as they ran for bandages and medication that was needed immediately rather than regularly. There was nothing of quiet in this place where people raged against the dying of the light.

Leaning against the wall of Drew's room in the ICU, Gwen folded her arms and thought that the sounds in Intensive Care were the worst in the hospital. The quiet was filled with tension. No patients screamed or wailed here; their bodies were either too sedated or too damaged and had no energy for anything but the silent internal struggle to hold on to life.

Visitors sat quietly, occasionally releasing stifled sobs into tissues pressed close to their mouths, for fear that if they let their emotions cry out the invisible death that drifted behind the nurses in the corridors would hear them and start to focus on their loved ones. Machines beeped, just like the one attached to Drew, and time was marked out by the too-regulated huff and puff of ventilators. The living mocked the dead with their stillness, and under the soft quiet of those that were conscious and the beeps and hums of machines was the awful crackle of tension. The noises where the difference between life and death was as fragile as a gossamer strand were the worst of the building. They tore strips from the soul.

Gwen let out a long sigh. At least they'd secured Drew a private room. The infirmary was overcrowded and, according to the nurse, tonight was a busy night for those intent on dying. Behind one of the curtained cubicles, a 34-year-old man was heaving up the bottle of paracetamol he'd swallowed an hour or so earlier before changing his mind about just how bad his life was. He seemed to think he would be OK but, coming back from the coffee machine, Gwen had seen the looks on the doctors' and nurses' faces. They were placing their bets on kidney failure setting in by morning. She'd seen that look before. God, it was all so depressing.

The coffee sat cooling on the small table beside her. She'd taken one sip and that was enough. It tasted like crap. But then she supposed coffee wasn't high on anyone's priorities in this part of the ward. The machine attached to Drew released another soft beep as his ventilator continued to steadily pump air down past his damaged throat and into his lungs and then pause to let it out again.

She wondered if he was dreaming in his sedated sleep and whether he was stuck in a nightmare of watching the alien that attacked him ripping apart his boyfriend. He wouldn't be having it for long at least. As soon as he was recovered enough, they'd Retcon him. Still. Serial killer. Alien. Either way it wasn't going to make much difference to his grief.

The door clicked open, and Ianto stepped inside. He looked tired, and a dark shadow of bruise oozed out from under the taped gauze covering the stitches running across his temple.

'I thought you'd gone home.' Gwen squeezed his arm. 'You might have concussion.'

'Well, if I do then I'm in the right place.' He looked at the coffee. 'That going spare?'

'Yes, but I wouldn't recommend it.'

Ianto leaned against the wall beside her and for a moment neither spoke, lost in their own quiet worlds.

'I saw the doctor.' Ianto's voice was barely more than a whisper, its deep tones just reaching Gwen's ears. 'They're going to move him to a recovery ward tomorrow.'

Her heart thumping with relief, Gwen grinned. 'That's brilliant news. Bloody brilliant.' She was as relieved for her quiet colleague as she was for the man in the hospital bed. She knew there was nothing more he could have done against the alien, but Ianto would be having a harder job convincing himself, the same way she would if their roles had been reversed. If Drew had died, he would have seen it as his fault for messing up his job.

Ianto's eyes slipped to the man on the bed, his jaw set firmly. 'He'll never sing again, though.' He paused. 'He'll be lucky if he can talk.'

'But he'll be alive.' Gwen shivered at the cool monotone of Ianto's delivery.

'Singing *was* his life.'

She shook her head. 'No it wasn't. It was just part of it. A big part maybe, but not all.' Her mind wandered down the corridor to the man who, just hours before, had thought he was desperate to die and was now chucking his guts up for all he was worth in the vain hope he'd make it to the weekend and this would just be a story he could tell to his mates in the pub for a bit of a laugh. 'He'll be happy he's alive mainly.'

'Maybe. At first.' He frowned. 'Where's Jack?'

'Said he had some stuff to do.'

'What, back at the Hub?'

Gwen shook her head. She'd seen the grim set on Jack's face as the ambulance pulled away. 'I doubt it. He had that look.' Glancing up to Ianto, she watched him nod. He knew what she meant.

'We won't see him for a few hours then.'

'No.'

He sniffed. 'What were you planning to do? Go home?'

'If I went home this early, Rhys would go into shock. He's probably just opening a beer in front of the football.' The machine pinged again and she wondered what the point of it was. Maybe its purpose was just to momentarily relieve the oppressive hush of the ward and allow the occupants to breathe.

'So, what's the plan? Stay here all night?'

She shook her head. 'I thought I might take a look at the data from just before the attack. For a few seconds it seemed like there was Rift activity all over the city, then it suddenly spiked at the church. I'm going to see if there's any way to refine the program. Maybe we can get it to show us where the alien's going to appear with enough time for us to get there.' She gritted her teeth and, although she was staring at Drew, her mind had rewound to the moment they'd burst into the church. 'We were only round the corner, but if you hadn't distracted it we'd never have saved this poor sod.'

Ianto smiled at her. 'Refining the program, eh? Tosh would be proud. We'll make a geek of you yet.'

'I'm more likely to break the bloody monitor than get it working better. Still, I've got to try something.'

'You want a hand?'

Gwen smiled. 'Definitely. That way the blame gets split when we wreck the computer.'

TWENTY

The bar was dimly lit with various pink and blue neon strips running along the bench seating and under the chrome edge of the marble top that Jack was leaning his elbows on. The sleeves on his blue shirt were rolled up, and for once it felt like his braces were digging into his shoulders. Or maybe it was just psychosomatic. It sure felt like something was causing that tense ache that sat tight in his muscles and he'd rather think it was the braces than the alien.

Picking up his bottle of water he took a long swallow, avoiding looking in the mirror that lined the back wall. It was only partly hidden by bottles of spirits in the kinds of colours you just know are going to disagree with your insides, and his own face was one he could do without looking at right now.

'Have you got ten sets of that clobber or something?'

The stool next to him grated roughly on the floor as it was tugged out, and Jack looked up and smiled.

'Something like that.'

Cutler wore jeans and a V-neck sweater, the casual clothes suiting his scruffy hair and stubble. Sitting down, he nodded at the barman. 'JD and coke. Double.' He looked over at Jack who tilted his bottle. 'And another of whatever that piss-water is.'

'I thought you'd stood me up.'

Cutler snorted out a laugh and passed a ten pound note over to the barman. 'Yeah, right. Where else am I likely to be? Everywhere I go there's a phone ringing for me.' He picked up his drink and swallowed nearly half of it. 'Not too different for you either, I should imagine.'

'Ain't that the truth.'

They sat in silence for a moment, Cutler staring into the black liquid glowing slightly in the reflected light. 'We had a lucky escape today. If that poor bastard had died…'

'Yeah, I know.'

And Jack *did* know. It was easy for the brass above Cutler to start screaming at the DI about results, but it wasn't them out chasing the unknown and everything else that the Rift spat out in their faces. The world was angry and needed people to blame, and it was human nature always to look to others rather than themselves. Where would Earth be without Torchwood and the people that risked – and lost – their lives to keep the planet safe? He hated himself for the moment of bitterness, but sometimes it was just too damned hard. If only they understood just how much was really going on.

'It's the twenty-first century,' he muttered. 'And that's when everything changes.'

'What was that?' Cutler looked sideways.

'Nothing. Nothing relevant.' Jack sighed and stretched out his back. 'Nothing that can't wait. At least for a while.' He turned away from his reflection and looked into the tired face of the DI. 'I'm sorry we haven't gotten this taken care of quicker. It can't be easy for you.'

Cutler shrugged. 'I've seen that creature at work. Your team's doing its best. So no apology needed.' He drained his glass and signalled for a refill before catching the flash of concern that must have showed on Jack's face.

'Don't worry.' He grinned, but the expression was carved into his face, lacking the spontaneous warmth of someone undamaged. 'I'll take it slowly with this one. But at least allow the condemned man to see in the death of his career with a decent hangover.'

'Is it that bad?'

'It's not good. And neither is my track record if you believe what you read on paper, which of course my bosses don't, but it's the paper record that the rest of the world have access to. Hence the big worry back at HQ is what the press will make of it when they eventually start digging around on me.' His laugh was bitter. 'Better to ship me off to somewhere even more in the sticks than Wales.' He looked over at Jack. 'No offence.'

'None taken.'

'Although I'm not entirely sure what's left. The bloody Orkney Islands? Don't really see it for me.'

'You think they're going to fire you?' Jack watched him thoughtfully.

'Maybe. Hang me out to dry, definitely. They can't afford to take the flack.' He raised an eyebrow. 'This is a high-profile serial killer case. And I'm a DI with a big black mark on his record where killers are concerned.'

'I read your file.'

'So, you've read those papers then.' In the haze of blue neon light, Cutler's face had the smooth sheen of marble. Jack presumed his own looked the same. Perhaps it was apt for both of them. Men made of stone. He was unable to die, and Cutler had hardened himself against the world to the point where he seemed untouchable. Maybe that was the only way he'd kept his head.

'No.' Jack leaned in. 'I read your Torchwood file.' He paused. 'You did a very noble thing.'

'Oh yeah. And look how it paid off. My wife left me and my career's all but dead.' Cutler stared into his drink. 'Looking back, noble might not have been the best move.'

Turning on his chair, Jack studied the other man. 'So why did you do it?'

'What exactly does the file say I did?' Cutler's eyes were cool mirrors of defensiveness. 'I'm not a great believer in what can be read on paper.'

'It's pretty frank. It says you told the court that you

falsified evidence which stopped Mark Palmer going to prison for the sexual abuse and rape of three young boys.' He let a mouthful of water fizz against his tongue before swallowing. 'I checked out the newspapers too. Seems like he was definitely going down until you admitted that. He was looking at life with no chance of parole. Not that he would have lasted too long without a knife in the back in the rec yard.'

'That was my problem.'

'How do you mean?' Jack had read the file. He could figure out pretty much what had been going on in the policeman's head, but he wanted to hear it from him. He wanted to hear it from the Cutler that existed now, the man that had survived the aftermath of that decision. Making a choice was easy. It was the consequences that changed you.

'I couldn't let an innocent man go to prison.'

'Torchwood One was going to.' Jack felt no pride in that statement. 'And from what I read from the trial reports, Mark Palmer wouldn't have fought it too hard.'

'Palmer's head was too messed up to know what was going on.' The small muscle in the side of Cutler's head twitched at his temple, the only indication that under the calm voice, his emotions were raging. 'By the time he got to court he was half-convinced he *had* killed those boys. Even if he didn't remember any of the murders.'

Jack teased at the damp paper label on his water, peeling it slowly away, ignoring its reluctance to come free. 'You know, some people would argue that he wasn't really that innocent. That entity that invaded him simply acted out his desires. The things that were already longings in his head.'

Cutler shifted on the stool. 'God, I hate this smoking ban. How are you supposed to drink and relax without a bloody cigarette?'

Picking at the edge of the silver square, Jack pulled free a strip of the shiny surface declaring the water's brand, leaving a trace of white undercoat behind on the bottle.

'But what do you make of that theory?' He wasn't letting go. He needed to understand this man that Torchwood One had seen fit to leave without dealing with him in some way, relatively pleasant or otherwise. He needed to peel away the surface and see if he was indeed the same man that had existed then. Because the same decision was coming his way when all this was eventually over. And he wanted to make the right one if he was going to live with the consequences.

Cutler sighed. 'I think it's a pile of shit.' He sipped his drink. 'If you'll excuse the technical police term.'

'I speak Police.' Jack smiled. 'How come, though?'

'How come you're so interested?'

Jack didn't shift his gaze from the policeman's own but flashed him a brief dazzling grin. 'I'd just like to know a little bit about a man I'm heading to the scaffold with. And the records made me curious. You'd be the same.'

Where Jack's smile was all boyish excitement, Cutler grinned like a hungry wolf. 'Don't think I haven't done a little research on you.'

'What did you find?'

'A lot of password-protected, access-denied files in the system and some crazy stories on the net. Enough to let me know I don't really want to know what's going on with you.'

'Fair enough.' Jack pulled the final strand of the label free and tossed it on the bar to be swept away by the bartender. It was a quiet night, and Jack thought the young man looked bored out of his mind. It would be great if he could just have the occasional moment like that. He lived in a world within the world, just like Gwen and Ianto. Cutler, however, was in purgatory, stuck somewhere in between.

A lot of ordinary people got glimpses of the strangeness that the Rift created, but very few were forced to evaluate their own morality because of it. Jack had respected Cutler before he'd read the file. He was intrigued by the man now. It was a refreshing feeling.

'So, tell me about Mark Palmer.'

'I hounded him, you know.' Cutler stared thoughtfully at his own reflection in the mirror, and Jack wondered if he was looking for that ghost of the self he had lost a long time ago. 'After the first death, when the trail was leading back to him. Loner. Used to hang around the play area. Ideal suspect.' He frowned.

'I could smell it on him; his guilt. Those three boys died within four days and he couldn't remember where he was for any of the times the boys went missing. Before the bodies were found, I camped outside his house. I rang him day and night to stop him sleeping.' He paused and swallowed. 'I was a complete bastard. I watched him pacing up and down in his living room, his hands in his hair, and I'd call and call and call, and if he answered I'd tell him what I was going to do to him when we had him. All from a pay-as-you-go mobile in a dummied-up name, of course. No trace. No police harassment blame. Poor sod was already going half mad and I was sending him the rest of the way. And then, after a few days, it was me that thought I was losing my marbles.'

'What happened?'

'It was about midnight. Palmer came out of his house and was on his front lawn. He was really agitated. Talking to himself, twitching. I thought he was cracking. I thought I had him. And then suddenly he stood totally still. His back straightened and all that anxiety went out of him. I could see it from the car. He changed. And when he turned round and strode to his car I honest to God thought someone had slipped me something or maybe the case had got to me and *my* brain was frying. His eyes were wide open and it was like looking into headlights on full beam. Bright white light poured out of him. And from his mouth too, when he opened it. It was insanity, but I was seeing it.' Cutler sipped again at his drink.

'I followed his car, and he drove out to the woods where he parked up, hidden out of sight from the lane. He got out and took a shovel out of the boot before striding in this… over-controlled way into the darkness. I stayed pretty far behind, but those eyes lit up the way through the trees anyway, so I wasn't in any danger of getting lost. He was going to the bodies of course.

'He dug like a machine, which I guess he was, looking back. His body was being used by whatever was inside him and those boys weren't buried in a shallow grave. By the time he was done, he was sweating and panting but he kept going until that light poured out of him. Then he collapsed. I watched him crying over the bodies while that light leapt and whirled and ran in and out of the dead boys, touching them all over again. I couldn't move. It was beautiful, but at the same time there was such…' Cutler struggled for the right word. 'There was such *malevolence* in it. Human evil is so much more mundane than whatever that thing was. Once it was done with the fun it was having with the corpses, it went back into Palmer. He reburied the bodies and drove home like an automaton.'

'What did you do?'

'Didn't sleep. Didn't call it in. I knew where the bodies were, I'd marked the three trees around them once Palmer and the thing inside him had gone. I sat on the sofa, smoked a lot, and drank a lot. I thought about the truth. *The truth is out there*, kept going round in my head. Mulder and bloody Scully.' He laughed, a dry, dark sound, like disturbed mud.

'And then I went into work early and dug around in the system looking for whatever department had to deal with paranormal reports or out-of-the-ordinary crimes, and time after time "Torchwood: Classified" came up. I'd never heard of any section called that, so I kept digging and searching under that name. By 9.32, Torchwood staff and my DCI were standing at my desk wanting to know what my sudden interest was. And after a while, when my DCI had buggered off, I told them.

'And the rest, as they say, is history. The bodies were found, Torchwood caught the entity or whatever that shite was inside Palmer, and a line was drawn under the whole thing.'

'Except,' Jack cut in, 'all the evidence still pointed to Palmer. And the press had got hold of that.'

'Yeah, some bastard constable leaked it. Thought we weren't moving fast enough on the arrest.'

'Which you were busy trying to find a way to avoid.'

'Yeah.' The barman replaced their drinks, though Jack couldn't remember seeing Cutler signalling for fresh ones. Maybe their expressions said enough for the man to know they'd settled in for the night. 'But then it was all over. People were screaming for his arrest, and as all the DNA evidence clearly stated that he was guilty our hands were tied. We arrested him. Poor bastard was a mess. And I understood why. When I'd first been watching him, so bloody convinced I had my man, I knew he was *wrong* on the inside. But what I had been too busy to notice was that Palmer knew it too. He'd known it all his adult life, I imagine. Yes, he wanted to hurt those boys and do things to them that you and I just can't comprehend, and yes, he wanted to squeeze their lives away with his bare hands. He'd wanted to do things like that for as long as he could remember. In his head he was a sick bastard. But it was only in his head.'

Pausing, Cutler ran one hand through his hair and looked at Jack. 'He never acted on his impulses. And I don't think he ever would have if that thing hadn't got inside him. He was too strong and he knew it was wrong. Imagine living like that. Hating yourself and your desires. No wonder he was a loner. The worst he ever allowed himself to do was sit and watch little boys playing in the park. He never talked to them. He never touched them.' He paused. 'Jesus. And then this thing comes along, gets inside him and wants to do it all. All those years of restraint, over. And all we can do is put him in prison for it?'

Watching him shake his head, his brow knotted tightly together, Jack wondered if Cutler realised how animated he'd become. Behind all those defences, Cutler's anger still raged and Jack was glad about that.

'You couldn't,' he said softly.

'You're right. I couldn't. But the evidence was too great against him. So I waited until the court was in full session and then started a rumour in the press about tampered evidence. Planting of DNA. All that shit. It started to circulate. And when I got called to the stand and the defence questioned me on it, I did a big pretence of breaking down and then confessed. Said the pressure to get a conviction had been too much. They had no choice but to throw it out of court. Civil action found him guilty but he didn't really have a lot to lose by then. We gave him a new identity and sent him north for a new life. Not that it worked. Last I heard, he was a drunk, and after three suicide attempts he was sectioned off into some mental hospital. Probably the safest place for him.'

'Would you do the same thing again?'

Cutler stared angrily into the mirror. 'Yeah. I think I'm that dumb that I probably would.'

'I'm surprised Torchwood One let you go so easily.'

Cutler shrugged. 'They thought I'd handled the situation well. No running to the press or even my boss with tales of bright lights in the night. They figured I'd be useful on the force. If I heard stories of anything strange.' He smiled. 'But believe me, I don't think it was an easy decision for them. Looking back, I sometimes wonder what they might have done if they had thought I was a liability. Being young and stupid at the time I didn't give it any thought. But now…'

'I think I can see why they left you the happy individual that you are.' Jack raised his bottle. 'Cheers.'

Cutler clinked his JD against the mineral water. 'Your curiosity satisfied?'

'A story's always better told than read. If it means anything at all, I think what you did was the right thing. And most people wouldn't have done it.'

'Thanks.'

'You were never tempted to tell your wife the truth?'

Behind them, the jukebox burst into life, pumping out Britney Spears's 'Toxic'.

'You learn about people in those situations. She

believed the lie too easily. Made me see her more clearly. She wasn't worth the truth.' He turned on his stool and stared at the source of the over-loud music. 'Jesus. Can't a man even have a drink in peace and quiet? Why do we have to fill every thinking moment up with noise? All I bloody want is a couple of minutes of silence to let my brain get things in order.'

Jack began to smile, and then froze. *A couple of minutes of silence*. He pushed the stool back and punched the bar, the thud full of vigour.

'You gotta love that Britney!' His eyes sparkled and, with his grin bubbling energy, he leaned forward, grabbed Cutler's cheeks in his hands and planted a loud kiss on his lips. 'Two minutes of silence! You're a genius! Why didn't I think of that?' He grabbed his long coat from the seat on the other side and then stared at Cutler. 'What are you waiting for? Come on. Let's go catch the bad guy.'

The detective stared at him for a long second before standing up. 'I've got no idea what you're on about, but I'm coming.' He drained his glass. 'And if you ever kiss me again I will have to terminate this working relationship with a knee in your bollocks.'

Jack's laugh danced behind him as he ran up the stairs from the basement bar and up to the pavement. 'Say what you like, I'm a great kisser. You loved it. I can tell.'

'Bloody Torchwood,' Cutler grumbled, but Jack could hear the humour in the gruff voice. 'Can't do anything like *bloody* normal people.'

TWENTY-ONE

Jack paced slightly in front of the Boardroom table in a narrow area that wasn't designed to incorporate a huge amount of pacing. Energy and excitement had been sparking off him since he'd bounded back into the Hub with Cutler in tow and, although it was almost midnight, Gwen's own foot tapped under her seat. Jack obviously had news – there was no way he would have brought Cutler if it hadn't been something important – but so did she and Ianto.

'OK, so here's the new plan.' Jack finally stopped moving, letting Gwen's eyes focus. 'At 11 a.m. tomorrow, we're going to hold a city-wide, two-minute silence as a mark of respect for the deaths of Maria Bruno and the other victims.' He nodded towards Cutler, who was leaning against the corner of the wall. 'The police have been in touch with all the major news stations, and it's going to be hitting all the channels from now until daybreak.'

'You think the whole of Cardiff will take part?' Ianto was back in his suit, complete with jacket, and looking contained and smart despite the bandage across his head. He flashed Cutler a suspicious glance, and Gwen knew why. Jack had to think the man was pretty special if he had brought the outsider into the Hub. And she could recognise a jealous look when she saw one.

'They don't need to. Only the singers. Only the *good* singers.' Jack folded his arms across his chest. 'And they're the ones we need to do it.'

Gwen knew she was tired, but she wondered if she was missing something. 'So, if all the singers have shut up, how's that going to help us catch the alien?'

We can't afford to risk another civilian, but *we* have our own voice of an angel among us…' As Jack let the sentence trail off, Gwen turned to Ianto and waited for him to catch up. He did.

'I'm the bait?'

Jack grinned. 'If you're the only show in town, let's hope you'll be guaranteed an audience.'

'Great.' Ianto's expression disagreed with the word. 'An audience that rips your throat out if you sing too well.'

'We'll have the place covered and I'll be inside with you. And heavily armed.' Jack's grin had disappeared, his dark eyes intent. 'If we get the place rigged up right, he won't even get near you. You going to trust me on this?'

Ianto nodded. 'Of course.' His eyes sat quietly grim in his calm face. 'And we don't have any choice anyway. We have to do it.'

Gwen sat up in her chair, her impatience overtaking her. 'And you should have more notice of the creature's arrival this time round.'

'How come?' asked Jack.

Gwen grinned and glanced at Ianto, her own pride reflecting back at her from him. God, they were like children trying to impress their dad. But still, that was the truth. They both *did* want to impress Jack.

'While you two have been in the pub, we've been pretty busy here, and not just eating pizza.'

'Although I saw the box.' Jack raised an eyebrow. 'You did *have* pizza.'

'Smart arse. We ate while we worked.' She pushed her dark hair away from her face. 'Anyway, just before Drew Powell was attacked, do you remember that I saw all those tiny flashes that appeared randomly across Cardiff on the Rift monitor? Just before the big one at the church?'

Jack nodded. 'Go on.'

'It got me curious, so I looked at the data for the other attacks. We'd seen there was a big spike just before each one, but because we were looking with hindsight—'

'Retrospectively.'

'Whatever. Means the same.' She glared at Ianto. 'Because we were studying the attacks *retrospectively*, we hadn't looked to see what activity went on just prior to the main Rift spike. So I went back a bit further.'

185

A smile twitched at the corner of Jack's mouth. 'You've been working on a computer all night? Is this the same Gwen Cooper who runs at the sight of a USB cable?'

'It's the same Gwen Cooper who'll forget what she's trying to say if you're not careful.'

'Keep going.' Jack's eyes twinkled. 'I'm impressed.'

'OK, these outbreaks of tiny spikes were there just a minute or two before each attack, as if maybe the alien comes through in particles or something and then pulls itself together. But whatever the reason, what we found was that the tiny spikes aren't random. It's like a reverse explosion. The centre point between them is where the alien appears.'

'Good work,' Jack said, but Gwen shook her head.

'I haven't finished. That's not the good bit.' She leaned forwards slightly, her elbows digging into the table. 'Ianto and me have refined the system so that it picks up those early spikes more quickly and gives us the appearance location before the creature comes through. Should buy you about eight minutes, we reckon.'

Ianto nodded. 'Judging from our test runs.'

Jack stared at Ianto and then back at Gwen. 'You two figured this out yourselves?'

Gwen shrugged. 'With quite a lot of help from Tosh's notes and bloody pop-ups.'

'She'd be proud of you.'

Gwen couldn't fight the smile threatening to stretch across her face. 'Or horrified. She was probably watching over our shoulders making sure we didn't break her precious computer. It was her favourite member of the team.'

Jack grinned. 'She definitely thought it was more logical than the rest of us. And I think I'd agree with her on that.'

Even Ianto gave a half-smile. Cutler stayed out of it, against the wall. This was their business, the sharing of a memory of a lost colleague. Gwen felt warm in her stomach, even if she knew the image was a childish fantasy. When you were dead, you were dead; there were no ghosts of Tosh or Owen watching over them. And if one day there was, it would just turn out to be some bloody alien or entity using their memories as a weapon against them.

Still, she thought. It was what they had signed up for. It was the risk they took for the rewards of all this knowledge and excitement. She glanced at Cutler. She couldn't go back to the police now. She could never turn her back on all this, not willingly, however much of her soul it took.

'So what now?' Ianto asked.

'There's nothing we can do until morning.' Jack looked at Gwen. 'That enhanced program up and running now?'

She nodded, and he looked over to Cutler.

'Your men still out in their patrol cars?'

'Oh yeah. I think I just drained the overtime budget for the next ten years on this one.'

Nodding, Jack sighed. 'That's about all we can do for

now then. You two go home and get some rest.' Both Gwen and Ianto moved to speak, but Jack cut them off. 'No arguments. I'll keep an eye on things here. If our visitor decides to make an appearance I'll at least have a few minutes to get the sirens to its location.' He looked at his watch. 'Although anyone singing at this time of night must be crazy.'

'There's one more thing.' Ianto frowned a little. 'It's just something I felt when the alien came for Drew Powell.' He looked up. 'I had this awful sense of emptiness. Loneliness, but human loneliness taken and multiplied a thousand times. It was so strong I can't explain it. I felt like I was being emptied of everything that I'd learned from outside of myself. Anything I'd been taught by anyone else, or shared with anyone else or *felt* for anyone else.'

He kept his head down while he spoke, never comfortable with talking about his inner emotions. 'But I didn't feel any aggression. Maybe frustration, but no aggression.'

'So what are you saying?' Jack frowned. 'You got to see inside the alien's mind?'

'Something like that. Or its mind invaded mine. That feels closer to it.' He looked up. 'All I'm saying is that I don't think it's killing these people on purpose. I don't think it really understands about killing. I'm not sure what it's doing, but the deaths aren't intentional.'

There was a moment's silence, then Cutler sniffed derisively from his position against the wall. 'I'm sure that will be a great comfort to the victims and their families.'

Gwen glared at him. He was a policeman right to the core. She remembered that kind of black and white thinking. There was no place for it here, even though she sometimes wished it were that easy.

'Maybe not.' Jack had the final word. 'But it might just help us when we catch it.'

TWENTY-TWO

Even at the edge of the void, the night was coated in quiet. Disembodied, it could feel the echo of pain where the metal had pierced its flesh. The pain and the metal and the addictive sensation of the physical were gone now, but the taste remained.

At least here, hidden in the breathless strangeness that had brought it so far from the silence of home, it could make out the gentle hum of the noisy world so close by. It sucked the sounds in, even though they weren't what it wanted or what had called to its despair.

The parts it had absorbed refused to function as they had in their original locations, and the rage of frustration bubbled out from the shapeless form and, somewhere outside the rim of nothing, a random bolt of lightning struck the surface of the peaceful sea. Fear rippled through its consciousness. Something was trying to pull it back across the universe, to correct the error *that had brought it here. There wasn't much time left to take what it needed. Alert and ready, it waited.*

In the Havannah Court Autism Centre, sleep had claimed Ryan Scott several hours earlier, his throat resting as his body shut down. He didn't move throughout the night, his small muscles relaxed and face peaceful; finally at rest in a black oblivion where he didn't have to be anything at all. Where he simply existed, self-contained and completely detached from those who disturbed him with their touches and their noises and their refusal to let him be alone. His chest moved up and down, air silently passing through the mechanics of his small form as he dreamed of blissful nothing. If he was capable of loving anything at all, Ryan Scott loved the night.

Sitting on the side of his oversized double bed in his suite in the St David's Hotel, Martin Meloy's nose ran in a constant stream. His eyes blurred with tears and he hiccupped out a sob before tilting his head back and trying to get control of his emotions. He needed to write this. His hand shook and he stared at the half-empty bottle of pills and the vodka bottle littering his bedside table. He didn't have a lot of time. 'I'm sorry,' he scribbled on the fine textured paper with the hotel's name and address embossed on the top.

He squeezed out a few more words before lying back on the bed, the paper balanced on his chest. His eyes drifted shut and he thought of his Mary Brown, who'd transformed herself into the great Maria Bruno, and hoped she would approve. He may never have been dramatic enough for her in life, but he hoped his death would be Hollywood enough for his gorgeous, glamorous, talented wife. His breathing slowed.

Adrienne Scott had drunk too much, and her head pounded as she crawled out of bed and headed to the kitchen. Not waiting for the tap to run deliciously cold, she filled the glass and drained its lukewarm contents greedily before letting it overflow again. She drank the second more slowly, a shaking hand finding the paracetamol easily in the dark. She'd had plenty of practice. Swallowing the pills, she stared blearily out of the kitchen window and into the night sky. Life couldn't go on like this. And it was visiting day tomorrow. Crawling back into her bed, relieved that there were at least three or four more hours of darkness before she had to move, she wished the idea of seeing her son didn't fill her with so much dread.

High above the Millennium Centre, Jack Harkness let the rain run through his hair as he watched over the city, standing firm; his jaw set and eyes grim.

And, slowly, the clocks of Cardiff ticked round to dawn.

TWENTY-THREE

The Church of St Bartholomew was a little way back from the hum of traffic on Lloyd George Avenue but still quite near the busy centre of Cardiff Bay. Jack figured there wouldn't have been enough hours in the night to search through all the potentially perfect rehearsal spaces, and this one ticked most of the right boxes. It was up to Ianto's voice to bring the alien to them, after all, and it seemed it could turn up pretty much anywhere. Still, the church had a certain charm, he had to admit, and outside the traditional grey structure the grounds were filled with enough leafy trees to provide a sense of protective cover, but not so many that each couldn't be watched for movement by the well-placed armed police units placed carefully both in the car park and the roads immediately surrounding it.

From the inside, Jack looked up at the decoratively stained windows. There were five at the front of the building and four down the side of each wall.

'If it wants some glass to play with,' he muttered, 'I'll give it glass.'

He gritted his teeth and scanned the edges, locating the small charges rigged at the corner of each window designed to go off on impact with the glass, not to kill the alien but to send it tumbling in the direction Jack wanted it to go, disorienting it enough for him to trap it when it landed.

He checked his watch and felt a buzz of excitement flutter through his stomach. 10.50. Almost now or never time.

Ianto was checking the CD backing track for what seemed like the thousandth time since they'd arrived, his finger clicking play, then stop, then play, over and over.

'You ready?' Jack smiled at him. 'You're on in ten.'

For once, the press had done what it was told and the two minutes' silence had been advertised on all news programmes and radio shows. Even the other judges had announced that they would expect all the contestants in the show, whether they had reached the finals or not, to honour the silence and remember the dead. Rehearsal spaces were staying locked all over town. As much as any one person could control the volume of Cardiff, Captain Jack Harkness currently had his finger on the remote control.

'I'm ready.'

Jack touched his earpiece. 'Gwen?'

'I'm ready. Although what I'm doing stuck here when all the action is out there…'.

Jack didn't have to see her to know that she'd be on her feet behind the desk, leather jacket zipped up, eager to be out in the field rather than Hub-bound.

'Hey, you amended the program, so you're the best one to operate it.'

'I should have done the work on the remote computer instead of here.'

'Well, it's too late for that now.' He grinned. 'And if you ask me, the geeky thing is working for you.'

'Yeah? Well, don't get too excited, I'm never wearing that white coat and glasses.'

'Shame. It's a sexy look.'

'Sod off, Jack.'

He laughed. 'Just stay in touch. Soon as you see any activity, I want to know about it.'

'Got that.'

Disconnecting, he checked his watch again. Five minutes to go.

'I don't mind going back to the Hub and wearing the white coat.' Standing still in front of the altar, Ianto looked nervous, one hand tugging at the sleeve of his shirt.

'You look best in a suit.' Jack winked.

'I thought you'd say something like that. Is it time?'

'Couple more minutes.' He pressed his earpiece again. 'Cutler?'

The gravelly London voice came straight back at him.

'Here. Out in the bastard rain. All quiet so far.'

'Good.'

Jack took a deep breath. All the preparations were done. All they could do now was sing and hope for the best.

Cutler leaned back in his seat and sighed. The window of the car was open so he could clearly see anything that might appear out of the grey skies or from behind the trees and bushes, and rain splattered his face in fine drops carried on the wind. His nerves jangled and he resisted the urge to light a cigarette. If only he had some idea of where and how the alien might appear, at least then he could focus. It seemed that right now he could use a spinning head like that girl from *The Exorcist* had. It was the only way he was going to see everything that was around him.

Movement in his wing mirror made his heart leap for a moment, and then he frowned, more wrinkles appearing in his already crumpled face. The figure wandering down the quiet street wasn't an alien. Well, technically not, but the next best thing to one as far as DI Cutler was concerned.

'Bloody students,' he muttered under his breath.

The girl with the long dark hair was definitely one of Cardiff's university types, he had no doubt about that. She was short, and her hair was tied back in an untidy ponytail, the Indian style chiffon scarf out of place against the rock band T-shirt that flashed under her tatty denim jacket as she strolled past his car. 'Franz Ferdinand' flashed in glitter against the black fabric, the letters coming and going with every stride.

He sighed. She was singing along to something pumping directly into her ears from an iPod or some such other under-25s' device. Her voice wasn't too bad against the pattern of the rain, but the rock music wasn't anything he recognised, although it did have a familiar sound. Maybe U2.

Singing.

'Hell.'

Grumbling at his bad luck, Cutler climbed out of the car, the rain immediately trickling down the back of his shirt and bringing a spine-shiver with it. He trotted forward, taking only a few steps to catch up with the girl, who had stopped and pulled her phone out of her pocket, texting happily, seeming oblivious to the chill and damp. No wonder he hated students. They were always so bloody young and full of optimism and ideals. No grown-up grumpy bastard like him needed that.

Cutler tapped her on the shoulder and her narrow frame jumped slightly, but at least she stopped singing. The last thing they needed was the alien going for another civilian, and, if it did, he didn't want to be the only one around. Having seen its handiwork, he didn't fancy his chances.

Her eyes clouded suspiciously in her pale face as she tugged the headphones out. Tinny music hummed in the air between them.

'Yes? Can I help you?'

'I'm going to have to ask you to leave the area as quickly and quietly as you can, miss…?'

'Nina.' The girl's suspicious expression was hit by a tidal wave of puzzled curiosity. 'Nina Rogers.' She raised an eyebrow. 'And you are?'

'Police.' He rummaged in his jacket and tugged free his ID. 'Detective Inspector Cutler.'

'So, what's going on, Mr Cutler?' She grinned cheekily. 'Are you on a stakeout?'

He forced himself to smile back. The girl was engaging, but this wasn't the time or the place for dealing with bloody youthful enthusiasm. He walked forward, forcing her to subconsciously match his pace. 'Something like that. Now, if you could just head back to uni or your digs or wherever you're going, then I'd be grateful. And without the music.'

She frowned, and he could see her gearing up for another question.

'Now.'

His gruff word cut her off and, although he could see she was still curious, she did as she was told and, with a smile and a wave goodbye, she picked up her pace and headed back towards the main street.

Cutler watched her until she was safely round the corner and, satisfied that she'd left the music off, he climbed back into the warmth of his car. The problem with the young was that they had no fear. They'd learn, though. Everyone did.

Feeling his own fear dancing with nerves in the pit of his stomach, he sat back, stared out of the window, and waited.

TWENTY-FOUR

Adrienne Scott's head was thumping, and even though she'd got up for water in the night she still felt as if her tongue was glued to the roof of her mouth. It probably wouldn't have been so bad if she'd stopped after the bottle she'd shared with Katherine in the pub, but instead she'd come home and opened another one. It had seemed like a good idea at the time, but she was regretting it now.

Pulling up a chair, she sat by the window and watched as Ceri eased Ryan's arms out of the stripy, long-sleeved T-shirt that he'd managed to get most of his breakfast down. Eating and singing didn't go together and, since Ryan wouldn't stop one, Ceri had to virtually shove the food into his throat to force him to swallow as a reflex while doing the other. Ryan ate a lot of soft foods. And Adrienne avoided visiting at mealtimes. It was hard enough accepting Ryan's unusual ways as it was. She wasn't cut out for the messy stuff. Even with her own son it made her feel sick. But then that was hardly a surprise. She was, after all, a *bad mother*.

As the nurse tugged the clean top over his small blond head, the volume of Ryan's song increased, maybe hinting at some anxiety within, but even then he was note perfect.

Adrienne flinched and rubbed her head. The noise wasn't helping her hangover, regardless of how in tune his rendition of 'Walking In The Air' was. Trying to ignore the tremble in her hand as she reached for the cup of sweet coffee Ceri had made her, Adrienne wondered how many times Ryan had worked his way round that CD in the two days since her last visit. She was surprised Ceri hadn't been driven mad.

The shirt on, Ryan's singing reverted to its normal level, the little boy's perfect blue eyes staring straight ahead at nothing. He hadn't glanced her way since she came in, but that came as no surprise. He never acknowledged her. Maybe she should just stop coming.

She'd suggested as much to Ceri once, and the nurse had just smiled at her and said that was her prerogative but it wouldn't happen. Adrienne had asked her why, and Ceri had said because Ryan was her son and, as much as she might not always know it, she loved him. Adrienne had wanted to laugh out loud at that.

Letting her hangover throb, Adrienne looked at the little boy sitting in the middle of the room, ignoring his toys and singing so perfectly. Did she love him? Could she love him? How could you love someone that refused to accept anyone else's existence and gave no sign of any recognition, even of his own mother? How could she pour love into a child like that?

Sighing, she turned her gaze to the window and out into the rain. They were thoughts for another time, when she wasn't feeling quite so rough. Still, it was nearly eleven and time to go, her penance done for another day. Trying unsuccessfully to zone out the singing, she stared at the grey skies and sipped her coffee.

Alone in the Hub, Gwen watched as the hands on the large round face of the clock ticked on to eleven o'clock. This was it. The silence had started. Her heart thumped loudly in her chest, defying the command for quiet, and she chewed her lip as she stared at the screen.

Come on, she thought. *Come on*. Patience was not her strongest point, and she fought the urge to kick the machine. A mile or so away, Ianto would be launching into song; him, Jack and Cutler all waiting for information from her. Her stomach flipped. What if she hadn't made it work better? What if she'd actually messed it up?

Clenching her teeth, she tossed her hair angrily over one shoulder. This was why she hated being stuck at the Hub. There was too much bloody thinking time. Out in the field where she belonged, you didn't have time to think. You just *acted*. And it was easier that way.

There was too much helpless responsibility back here.

What if something went wrong? Was she just supposed to sit here and listen in while the alien ripped her friend apart? She huffed under her breath. This was the first and last time she'd ever let herself have any clever technical ideas. And if she *did* have any more, then she'd bloody well keep them to herself. If there really had been a ghost of Tosh watching over her, then the other woman would probably be laughing right now. Gwen had none of Toshiko's cool, methodical thinking. Maybe Tosh's spirit had planted the idea in Gwen's head in the first place as some kind of beyond-the-grave joke. Maybe she and Owen were rolling around invisibly giggling at her on the Hub floor. Even though she didn't believe in life everlasting or hauntings on Earth, alone and nervous as she was, Gwen still found the idea a little creepy.

Something on the screen flickered, and the imagined ghostly laughter stopped. A tiny spike flashed to the far right of Cardiff Bay.

This was it.

The alien was coming.

Two more small spikes flickered in and out of existence. She touched her earpiece.

'Jack?' Her voice was too loud, echoing back at her in the empty basement building. 'It's starting.'

Standing up, she folded her arms across her chest and willed the machine to spit out the appearance location.

Three more small spikes appeared, and then finally the red light she'd been waiting for glowed, the map automatically zooming in to highlight the address.

Gwen frowned. But that couldn't be right. That wasn't where Jack and Ianto were. Her hand went back to her earpiece.

'Jack. We've got a problem.'

TWENTY-FIVE

His voice filled the church and, although the baritone wasn't supposed to sing the piece alone, Ianto was making it work as best he could. Jack was surprised at the richness of the sound and the power carried in it. He was impressed. But then Ianto had proved himself several times over to be quietly full of surprises. Gwen's voice cut into his thoughts.

'Jack. We've got a problem.'

'What do you mean?'

'It's coming, but not to you. The computer says it's going to Havannah Court. The Havannah Court Autism Centre.'

Looking up at the iconic images of the saints that peered down at him from the undamaged stained-glass windows, Jack fought an urge to scream. 'Are you sure?'

'That's what the bloody computer says.' She paused. 'Hell.' Gwen's voice sweated urgency in his ear. 'We've got less than eight minutes, Jack. I'm closer than you. I'll meet you there.'

'I'm on my way.' Running up the aisle towards the door, Jack heard Ianto's voice waver behind him. Not that it mattered. 'Havannah Court!' he called over his shoulder. 'I'll go with Cutler!'

Outside the rain lashed him with wet streaks, as if nature itself were siding with the alien and the Rift to foil their attempts to stop the chaos. His legs pumping, he raced towards Cutler's unmarked police car. They had no more than six minutes left. They weren't going to make it. Yanking the door open, he leapt inside.

'Why can't anything ever go according to plan?' Cutler demanded as Jack slammed the passenger door shut.

'Welcome to Torchwood.'

Cutler fired up the engine and the tyres squealed, burning against the tarmac.

Ryan had moved from 'Walking In The Air' to 'Where Is Love?' and was now starting 'Close Every Door' from *Joseph and the Amazing Technicolour Dreamcoat*. The room filled with the mournful quality of the opening notes and, looking out into the trees and gardens of the centre, Adrienne idly thought that Jason Donovan would never have been able to come close to the emotionally perfect delivery her boy gave it. She should make a move and head to chambers where there was a stack of work waiting for her, but outside the heavens had opened, and she thought she'd wait for the downpour to slacken before leaving. She could only imagine what the receptionist would have to say to the nurses otherwise. *That eager to leave she got herself soaking wet. And her a barrister too. It's a crying shame. Bad mother.* Why give them the ammunition? And, to be honest, her hangover was still that bad, she couldn't bring herself to move from the chair. Her body felt like there was a lead weight in it. Driving had been no fun earlier, and she'd thought an abrupt brake might make her throw up all over her steering wheel.

Something shifted in the trees outside and, her eyes drifting and only half-focused, Adrienne waited to see a bird fly away in search of twigs to nest with or worms for its babies' hungry mouths. Nothing emerged, but the branches shook again, with more energy than the first time, as if someone were violently forcing its fruit to fall. Frowning, the throb in her skull for a moment forgotten, she leaned forward. Was there someone in there? Why the hell someone would be up a tree in this weather she couldn't guess, but then, with the children at the autism centre, you could try for ever and you'd never know their reasoning. She stared. Surely the nurses wouldn't let the children out to play in this weather.

'Ceri,' she said softly. 'I think there's a child in that tree.' She pointed at the swaying and jerking branches. 'See?'

Coming alongside her, the nurse nodded, her face puzzled. 'That doesn't look right. I'll bet it's Peter Allwood. He loves sneaking out into the grounds. I'll go and check.' Bustling out, she closed the door behind her, and Adrienne was about to look away from the grounds when a stream of dark shadow oozed out from the branches like a thick tendril of smoke. As her breath held itself locked in her chest, Adrienne's mind went blank as it scanned itself for any clue or explanation as to what was causing it. It came up with nothing. The cloud of blackness hung alone between the earth and sky, until another ghost of emptiness emerged, creeping round from the back of the tree to meet up with the first, two dark snakes intertwining and becoming one. Adrienne stared, her mouth falling open. That wasn't a child in the tree. This was something else. Something strange. Something *other*.

Her brain felt like glue, and she briefly glanced back at Ryan, oblivious on the floor. Oblivious to what, she wondered, curious at her own choice of words, and then her eyes turned back to the shadow forming against the backdrop of the old oak tree, the darkness that seemed to leak like rotten sap from within the space between its limbs. *Oblivious to that.* Something flashed at the core of the black mass as it seemed to jerk and writhe, pulling itself into some kind of solid form. Adrienne's breath formed steam on the window and, watching the thing in the rain on the other side, she wondered if she should try to scream or call out. But she couldn't find the mechanics in her chest.

Behind her, her baby was still singing. *Her baby.* Those words stayed solid in her head, fighting the flow of language and thought that fled her mind, leaving it hollow with only herself to fill it.

Her baby. The thing was coming for her baby. And in that thoughtless moment, Adrienne Scott realised she loved her son very much.

Gwen pressed her foot down on the accelerator so hard that the pedal was in danger of bursting through the floor of the car. Horns blared as she weaved dangerously through the traffic, cutting across cars coming the other way with so little space to spare she could almost smell the shavings of their paintwork. Fighting the urge to squeeze her eyes shut, she pulled out to overtake a van and hoped she'd make it past. Holding her breath until she was back in her own lane, an orchestra of yells and curses coming at her from every driver's window, she glanced at the clock. Thirty seconds until the eight minutes were up.

Pulling into Havannah Court, the colourful sign of the autism centre just about visible at the other end of the road, Gwen wanted to scream and beat the steering wheel.

She wasn't going to make it. Damn, she wasn't going to make it.

Her baby.

Somewhere in the corner of her vision, Adrienne saw Ceri emerge onto the wet lawn, first of all looking at the tree, and then freezing as she caught sight of the black shadow that was moving towards the building, changing its shape as it did so. The nurse turned and fled. Standing on the other side of the glass, Adrienne didn't blame her. She knew she was breathing because of the damp mist blurring the window, but she couldn't feel the air moving through her lungs. She couldn't feel anything except the awful isolation coming from the creature on the lawn.

And it was a creature now.

The writing mass had pulled itself together, solid patterned limbs almost human under its bald scarred head. *Almost human.* If Adrienne had still understood the concepts of sanity and insanity, she would have thought she had finally flipped, or all the wine she'd drunk was making her see things, or come up with some other vain, desperate attempt at rationalising the monster coming towards her, but those concepts had fled when the terrible isolation invaded. If it wasn't for Ryan, she would have slipped silently and forgotten, even by herself, down the wall and into a heap on the carpet.

Ryan. Her baby. Those words carved themselves into her skull, fighting to stay acknowledged in the growing chasm of nothing. She loved him. *When there was nothing left, that became so obvious.*

Lifting her arms, their weight like dead flesh, she spread them wide across the thick glass. It wanted her baby. She could feel it in every cell in her body. Fighting the emptiness that threatened to consume her, she met the red glare from the monster's eyes and she felt the hum in the air as it prepared to come at her. She didn't need words to know these things. It was a mother's intuition.

The thing that faced her let out a silent roar that ripped at the very existence of her consciousness and, flinching against its power, the remnants of her individuality clung to the inside of her skull.

She stared through the glass.

Over my dead body.

For a moment there was stillness and, locked in that moment staring at each other, Adrienne thought that even the rain slowed, the drops hanging in the air, waiting and watching, sucked into the frozen conflict between monster and mother.

And then the creature tilted back its head and let the dark cavern of its mouth stretch horribly wide, exposing the empty nothing within; a darkness that would suck you in and lose you there, and Adrienne felt hot tears on her cheek.

The creature moved. And moved again, too quickly for her to see.

She squeezed her eyes shut.

Ryan.

And then the glass smashed.

TWENTY-SIX

Gwen's arms pumped, sweat and rain mixing on her face as she sprinted down the corridor of the autism centre. Somewhere up ahead, glass smashed. Nurses peered out from their rooms, the adult faces alive with curiosity and worry and the need to get involved.

'Get back inside and shut the doors!' Gwen yelled at them, dimly aware of figures starting back as she shouted. 'Stay back!'

Following the narrow corridor, Gwen turned the corner, peering quickly into each room. Where the hell was it? Three doors down, right towards the back of the centre, she finally stopped.

Staring into the small room, she very slowly raised her hand to her ear. 'Jack?' she whispered. 'Hurry up. We've got a situation.'

'Oh my God.'

The voice made her jump and, turning, Gwen grabbed the woman's arm and pushed her gently but firmly away from the door. 'I told everyone to stay back. I need you to go and wait in the reception area.' Gwen hoped her own hand wasn't trembling too much. Blood rushed through her veins, its content almost pure adrenalin.

'I'm his nurse.' The woman's round face wobbled as she swallowed back shocked tears. 'I'm Ceri Davies, Ryan's nurse. He's severely autistic. I've cared for him ever since he came in. That… that woman's his mother, Adrienne. She was visiting.' She paused. 'Oh my God.' A hand went to her mouth and she stifled a sob. 'What is that thing? Is it going to hurt him? I can't leave him. I can't.'

Gwen rubbed the woman's arm. 'Stay here. We might need you.' She didn't answer any of her questions. She didn't have the answers. Leaving the woman leaning against the wall, Gwen peered slowly round the door and into the little boy's room. Nothing had changed.

The window was smashed, blown inwards with such force that some parts of it had sliced all the way through the smart-looking brunette who lay twisted and wrecked on the carpet. Her pale and manicured hand was separated from her wrist and a large fragment of thick glass was embedded just below her cheekbone, standing upwards and reflecting the vacant stare from her glassy eyes. Gwen didn't even think about trying to get closer and checking for a pulse. She didn't need anything but her eyes to tell her the boy's mother was very dead. Her blood was everywhere, a large, growing pool under her body, and huge splatters across the walls of the small room where her arteries must have severed as her heart was still beating, pumping the crimson fluid out to stick to every surface it touched.

Gwen looked at the small boy sitting cross-legged on the floor. His mother's blood had tarnished his straw-blond hair and a thin, shiny streak trickled down his cheek, but his smooth face remained impassive. He was singing, softly but perfectly, despite his dead mother lying so close by, and despite the awful creature that crouched in front of him, one hand extended, one thick finger touching his slim, small throat.

'He sings all the time.' The nurse had crept up alongside her. She stared at the devastation, the horror of it echoing in her soft whisper. 'He sings to keep the world out.' Gwen felt the woman's warmth close to her own and couldn't bear to move her back.

Heavy boots thumped out an urgent rhythm on the clinically hard-wearing carpet, and Gwen looked up to see Jack and Cutler running towards her. She raised a hand, turning her gaze back to the boy and the alien in the room. Instinctively, Jack slowed his pace and Cutler did the same, quietening their approach.

Silently stepping aside, Gwen let Jack see the situation for himself. His eyes would read it faster than she could explain it. Jack edged into the room, staying close to the wall, and Gwen followed him, her movements tiny, creeping an inch at a time closer to the scene.

'He's severely autistic,' she whispered to him. 'Sings all the time.'

Jack nodded. Slowly he pulled the portable prison device from his pocket. 'We need to get the kid away from him. I can't trap him when he's touching the boy. And aside from that he might slash his throat open.'

'I'm not feeling that emptiness Ianto talked about.' Gwen let Jack pull away from her. If they were going to distract the alien to get little Ryan they needed to be on different sides of the room.

'Neither am I.' Jack's voice was low. 'But then we're not used to this thing keeping people alive either.'

Gwen looked over at the woman's body on the floor. 'It didn't keep her alive.'

In the centre of the room, the alien tilted its head, the red beams of light pouring from the dark spaces in its head caressing the boy's still face. The uneven hole below opened and shut a few times and then eventually it spat out some sounds.

'The others stopped.'

The words sounded like they were being forced through water, garbled and bubbled with phlegm, and although the creature struggled to produce them their meaning was clear.

Gwen looked over at Jack. In the doorway, the nurse and Cutler appeared, blocking the exit. Jack didn't signal them back, nor did he signal to Gwen that he wanted to start any distraction manoeuvre in order to grab the boy. He frowned. Gwen knew that look. He was curious.

He stepped forward two paces and then tilted his own head.

'What do you mean the others stopped?'

The alien didn't look up from the boy, but rolled its head this way and that as if bathing in the sound.

'It called me.' The words were rough, no tone or resonance, barked out as if the sound was a crime against the creature's nature. 'So far away. The nothing brought me to the sound. It was beautiful.'

Jack moved slowly to the far side of the room, crouching down where he could see both the boy and the alien. The singing child had lifted his head, his eyes on the grotesque fractured and grey visage in front of him.

'Are you from the Silent Planet?'

The beams of red sharpened and lessened, the edges softening. 'My world has no name. There are no names. No sound. No sight. There is only yourself. For ever.'

Jack frowned. 'So why come here?' He edged an inch closer to the boy and Gwen could see the portable device in his hand. 'We must be your worst nightmare.'

The creature sighed, its mouth losing shape. 'I am…' It paused. 'I am wrong.'

'Why did you kill those people?'

There was a long moment where all Gwen could hear was the boy's singing. It was 'Pie Jesu'. It was a song she must have heard a hundred times before, but it had never moved her until now. If her heart hadn't been about to explode from tension, she thought, it might have broken with the sheer emotional quality of his voice.

221

'The sound. I want the sound.' The creature shook its head, and Gwen felt the air tremble with the weight of the movement. 'But the parts didn't work.' For the first time, the alien turned its attention away from the boy and towards Jack. 'When I took them and made them part of me, they wouldn't work. I couldn't make the sound. Only the words.'

For the first time, Gwen felt a wave of the awful loneliness Ianto had talked about sensing. The sheer despair and hollowness of being entirely alone.

'It's not the parts that make the sound.' Jack eased forward and was within reach of the boy. 'It's the person. Alive. We're not machines.'

The alien's hand hovered, and for a second it moved just the tiniest bit away from the boy's neck, the contact broken. Jack crouched ready to move, and Gwen prepared to take the boy from him and run.

'Look!' In the doorway, Ceri gasped out the word and pointed.

On the floor, Ryan had reached up, his small hand touching the alien's face.

Cutler cursed from the doorway, and Gwen shared his exasperation. The moment was gone. The alien was focused back on the boy again, its own hand once again touching his throat.

Ceri let out a small laugh. 'He's never done that. He's never touched *anyone*. He's never even shown any indication that he knows anyone else exists!' Clapping her hands together, she held them to her face with joy, as if there were no dead woman on the carpet and no alien seated in the middle of the room. Gwen stared at her and then looked over to Jack. He watched the boy and the alien for a long time and then slid the prison device back into the hidden pocket of his jacket before backing away.

'Jack?' Gwen frowned. What the hell was he doing?

Jack stood up. 'He's never done anything like this before?'

The nurse shook her head. 'Never. He just sings. Has done since he could speak. It keeps the world out.'

'What are you thinking, Jack?' Gwen tapped her foot. They needed to save the boy before this thing disappeared on them again.

He didn't look at Gwen, fascinated instead by the boy's hands on the alien's face. 'I'm thinking that these two are made for each other.'

'What?'

'It makes perfect sense. It will make them happier.'

'I'm out in the cold here, Harkness,' Cutler said from the doorway. 'Although this is Torchwood, so I don't know why I should expect any different.'

Jack looked from the alien to the boy and back again.

'Jack?' Gwen growled. It was one thing Cutler being out of the loop, but she was one of the team. And it didn't help that she had Ianto in her ear pushing to know what was going on.

'They need to become one. Look at them.' Jack's face carried a weight of seriousness that Gwen had only seen rarely, and always when he was struggling with a decision that went against all he believed about the sanctity of humanity. Gwen felt her own frustration ebbing away. Looking to the door, she saw Ceri was nodding.

'Yes.' She smiled. 'Yes.'

'What are we doing, Jack?' Gwen's eyes darted between the humans and the alien.

For the first time, Jack looked up at her and smiled gently. 'Don't you get it, Gwen? Here, this boy is different because he doesn't want the world. He *wants* the isolation; to be completely alone. He doesn't understand the concept of society, of company, of communication...' Jack didn't bother keeping his voice low, instead becoming more animated as he explained. 'Everything that is part of our world he hides from behind his singing.' He turned to Ceri. 'Have I got that about right?'

The nurse nodded, tears still making tracks and carrying her mascara down her cheeks.

'And I should imagine that on the Silent Planet our visitor here is their equivalent of autistic. He wants to connect with someone or something. That's why he followed the music.' He looked up at Cutler. 'And that's why he killed the best singers. For the power of emotion in their performance. To be able to share emotion.' He shook his head slightly.

'The terrible isolated loneliness Ianto felt...' Gwen felt understanding prickle on her skin. 'That was the alien's emotion. How it's lived all its life.'

Jack nodded. 'Awful, isn't it? Imagine no light, no sound, nothing but the essence of your being. No memories to cherish. No sense of love. To be reviled by any of your kind you tried to connect with. Totally alone.'

Gwen tilted her head. 'So what are you saying we do? Let him go? Send him back?'

'No. We need to make existence easier for both of them.'

'How?' Gwen frowned. She wasn't getting it.

'The boy needs isolation, and the alien needs something to make the isolation easier.'

'Just speak bloody English, Jack.'

'Instead of absorbing the vocal cords, it needs to absorb the whole child.'

Gwen felt stunned. 'You can't be serious. How can we let it do that?'

The dark and frustrating eyebrow rose. 'How can we not?'

'Because…' Gwen stepped forward. 'Because he's just a little boy. We need to get him away from that thing and send it back.'

Jack shook his head. 'Don't think of his life in your terms. This is hell for him. And if we send this creature back, then we're condemning it. Can you really live with that?'

'He's right.' Ceri whispered softly. 'It's what Ryan needs. His mother's dead. We haven't seen his father since he came in here. He has no one.' She paused. 'And he hates the world.'

'This is crazy.' Cutler shook his head. 'But it makes a crazy kind of sense.'

Gwen looked at the perfect child, his blond hair stained with his mother's blood, his tiny hands paying the fractured creature more attention than he'd ever given the woman that bore him. She saw the want in those hands, greedily drinking in the creature's dark years of emptiness as his young voice continued to steadily create the aching music so out of place next to the cooling, damaged body.

'It's pulling me back.' The creature gargled the words. 'You have nothing more to fear from me.'

'Tell me.' Jack crouched between them. 'Can you absorb the whole? Can you make the boy part of you? Without killing him?'

The creature nodded.

Jack looked over to Gwen. 'Agreed?'

'Agreed.' And she was. Cutler mumbled his yes, and Gwen didn't have to look at the nurse to know what she thought.

Jack smiled. 'Then do it.' Standing up, he joined Gwen against the wall.

The alien opened the cavern of its mouth and tilted its head backwards, stretching out its thick neck. The fractures in the smooth skull grew wider and Gwen stared, both fascinated and horrified, as its solid form began to disintegrate. Where Ryan's fingers touched its cheek, the chubby childish digits dissolved as they became one with the dark cloud that had only seconds before been a solid form, his particles lighter than the mass of the alien until the two sets danced into one thick

226

cloud. Gwen was sure she saw a light smile tickle his face just before it unravelled.

The dark shadow hovered above them for a perfectly still moment, and then it slid out of the window and was gone, disappearing into the sky, and the Rift, and the universe beyond.

The last strains of 'Pie Jesu' hung in the air like the memory of a taste just out of reach; the ghost of all the music that Ryan had used to hide from the world behind. And then eventually they were left in silence.

The clock on the wall ticked loudly, insisting that the world move relentlessly onward, and finally Jack smiled. 'Now there goes a big step forward in interplanetary relationships.' He winked at Gwen. 'I mean, let's face it. You can't get closer than those two are now.'

'Harkness?' Cutler leaned against the doorframe. Folding his arms across his chest, he nodded towards the nurse. Ceri wandered into the small room, looking out of the smashed window, her face a mask of awe despite the rain falling into her open eyes. 'I think she could use a stiff drink.'

'Oh, trust me, we can do better than that.'

'In the meantime,' said Cutler, pulling his mobile out of his pocket, 'I'll call my team to clean this up. Unless you have any objections?'

'Go ahead. We don't need her for anything.'

Gwen looked down at the glazed, resigned expression on the dead woman's face and wondered what she'd make of this outcome. She hoped she'd be happy for her child. She sighed. Not that it mattered. When you were dead, you were dead. This woman's worries were over.

Turning away, Gwen left the room and its horrific contents behind. It seemed there had been so much death lately. Suddenly she felt the urge to run back to the flat and curl up with Rhys and eat a Chinese takeaway on the sofa and pretend that everything in the world was all right. And, just for a few hours, it would be. Rhys had that effect on her. He might not be the most exciting man on the planet – which Gwen knew for a fact, since she worked for the man that must surely claim that title – but Rhys was the most dependable and he loved her, and at the end of the day what more could she want than that?

Jack squeezed her arm. 'You OK?'

'Yeah.' Clearing the dark cloud from her face, she smiled. 'Yeah. Just glad it's over.'

Leaving Havannah Court Autism Centre behind, for the first time in days Gwen was happy to feel the heavy drops of rain running through her hair.

TWENTY-SEVEN

Jack took a long swallow of his bottled water as the man scraped the bar stool next to his out and sat down.

'I thought you'd stood me up.'

Cutler grinned. He was still in his suit this time; the hour earlier and the mood lighter. 'Are you crazy? Wherever I go, there are phones ringing for me.'

Jack laughed. 'But this time I'm thinking they're all being a little nicer when you answer.'

'Maybe.' Cutler nodded at the barman. 'JD and coke and whatever that piss-water is he's drinking.'

Pushing a ten pound note across the bar, Jack forced Cutler's own cash out of the way. 'I'm getting these.' He looked over at the detective. 'Let's call it a farewell drink.' He paused. 'I take it you are leaving Cardiff? And not to go to the Orkney Islands?'

'You guess right.' Stuffing his money back in his pocket, Cutler leaned forward on the bar. 'I've been called back to London. Seems the stink around me is fading.'

'Congratulations.'

They clinked bottle to glass and the note rang clear around the half-empty bar. 'Thanks. Although congratulations aren't necessary, are they? None of this has anything to do with me.'

Jack watched him thoughtfully. 'But you solved the case and brought an end to the terror of the Cardiff Slasher.'

Cutler laughed. 'Oh yeah. Of course I did.'

'It's in the papers. It must be true. Maria Bruno's husband cracked under the pressure of their debts and her constant put-downs and threats of divorce and murdered his wife, cutting out the organs that were most important to her. But not before he'd practised on a few others first, scouring the streets of Cardiff dressed in a thick black cape, seeking out his victims and monstrously killing them. But his taste for blood had grown too great and, even after the ruthless execution of his own wife, Martin Meloy just couldn't stop.'

Jack widened his eyes, exaggerating the impact of his words; his voice full of Victorian carnival melodrama. 'And then, feeling Detective Inspector Cutler's carefully slung net closing in around him, and with his final murder attempt foiled, he took the coward's route and ended his own life, leaving only the pitiful note, "I'm sorry. It was all my fault."'

He raised an eyebrow and then his bottled water, saluting the policeman.

'If that's what the papers say, then it must be true.' Cutler rolled his glass around in his hands. 'I'm glad you find it funny.'

Jack sighed. 'Sometimes you have to look at the lighter side. If you don't, the darkness will drive you mad. Take that on board from one who knows.'

'Poor bastard Meloy.'

'No.' Jack shook his head. 'He's dead. This doesn't hurt him.'

Cutler didn't look so convinced. 'You know what *is* funny?' he said, eventually.

'Go on.'

Jack watched the crinkles and lines of the other man's face. There were plenty running their way across his forehead and down his cheeks that had no place there for a few years yet. None of them looked like laughter lines.

'Well, think about it. I stuck the knife in my career by pretending I'd planted evidence, and now I've resurrected my career by actually planting evidence to set up a dead man. There's trace DNA of Meloy's been found at every crime scene or on each body just in case anyone tries to prove him innocent.' He shook his head. 'And Torchwood forced my hand in both cases.' Running his fingers through the mess of sandy hair that topped his head, he met Jack's gaze. 'So you can congratulate me as much as you like, but we both know it's all bollocks. There's no real truth or justice here. It's all a mockery.

Just like last time.'

Jack shook his head. 'You're wrong. You don't think what happened with Ryan Scott and the alien was justice? And do you really think the world is ready for the truth about the Rift and everything else that's out there?' Cutler didn't answer. 'Of course you don't. If you did, you wouldn't have stayed quiet all these years. It's just not as easy as black and white and right and wrong, although sometimes my job would be a lot easier to live with if it were. Truth is all perception. The truth can change.'

'The real truth of things is always there, Jack. Underneath. You know it. You just make choices and hope they're the best ones.' Cutler smiled. 'And I respect you for that. But I'm not sure it's a code I can live by.'

They drank in silence, each lost in their own thoughts. It was Jack that cracked the moment.

'I can make it true, though.'

He looked sideways at the policeman.

'I can make it as if none of the truth happened and what the papers say is real.' He paused.

'We have something. It kind of soothes the memory. Wipes the crap away. And trust me, it's normally for the best.'

'So is that how you deal with inconvenient people like me down here?' Cutler shook his head. 'That won't make it any truer. It will just make it true to me. And that's a completely different thing. I'll keep my brain untampered with, if you don't mind. Bitter and twisted is the way I like to be.'

'I thought that's what you'd say, but it would be rude not to offer.'

'And I thank you for your offer.' Cutler pushed back the stool. 'Just need to take a trip to the little boys' room and then I'm going to buy you a goodbye drink. A proper one. With alcohol in it and everything.' He paused. 'You'd have been a good man to have on the force, Harkness.'

Jack grinned. 'I'll get them in, sir.'

'You do that.'

Twenty minutes later, Gwen stood in the doorway of the bar, her slim figured haloed by light and with her hands on her hips. It was only when she walked in that Jack saw the slight frown pulling two lines down between her eyebrows. He wondered if he'd still know her when those lines settled there. Everything was uncertain. Everything could change. How long did Gwen have? Would her breath of life be any longer than Tosh's or Owen's or all the others he'd seen die in the name of Torchwood? The inside of his mouth stung bitterly.

Gwen looked at the policeman slumped over the bar, his blond head resting in his hands. A snuffled snore squeezed out from between his face and the smooth surface.

'I take it that's not been brought on by drink?'

Jack shook his head. 'No.'

'Didn't think so.'

Ianto joined them, his own neat suit the antonym of Cutler's, whose shirt hung out at the back. 'Retcon?'

'Yep.' Jack stood up. 'I slipped it in his drink when he went to the bathroom.'

'How come?' Gwen's disappointment was clear, but Jack didn't want to hear it. He knew she'd liked Cutler. He also knew that seeing Cutler out cold on the bar was a little like having a premonition of her own future. If Torchwood didn't kill her one way, then there was always the possibility it would take her another. There were no guarantees for anyone. And Retcon was a kind of death.

'He's been in the Hub. Worked with us closely.' The muscle in Jack's jaw twitched painfully. Sometimes he hated the things he had to do in his job. 'If he was staying in Cardiff then maybe he'd have been useful, but they were transferring him back to London. He'd be too far away to monitor. He could cause problems.'

He'd chosen his words carefully, and fully expected Gwen to fly into a rage at him over describing Cutler in terms of 'usefulness'. She didn't, though. Instead, he looked up to find her watching him thoughtfully with her dark, beautiful eyes. In the smooth neon light, she looked very young, and Jack once again wondered at these people that would follow him into situations that might bring about their own deaths but never his. What did he do to deserve their loyalty?

'Probably the right thing,' she said at last.

'Where shall we take him?' Ianto peeled the body into a seated position, trying to secure one arm over his neck.

Jack pulled a set of keys from the sleeping detective's inside pocket. 'Back to his place.' He stuffed a small piece of paper into Ianto's free hand. 'The address is there. It's one of those new apartments down in the Bay.'

Ianto nodded. For a moment, he didn't move and Jack felt his impassive gaze scrutinising him. 'This was the right thing to do, Jack,' he said eventually. 'It was the only thing to do.'

Jack nodded. He knew it. But it didn't stop him feeling like he'd just killed a man, and a man he'd liked and respected at that. Cutler would be different after this, and maybe he'd be happier and maybe not, but Jack had taken that choice away from him.

Gwen folded her arms. 'Sucks being the boss, I bet.'

'You got that right.'

Leaning in, she gave him a sudden, impulsive hug, squeezing warmth into his soul. 'We'll be ten minutes. You'd better bloody be here when we get back. You're not the only one that needs a drink. Right, Ianto?'

The tall young man nodded, his face straining under the weight of the solid, sleeping body. 'I will do once I've got him back home.' He shifted, trying to balance. 'He's heavier than he looks.'

'And anyway,' Gwen added with a grin. 'It's a week till pay day. So you're buying.'

Following Ianto, she was halfway to the door when she paused. 'You are OK, aren't you, Jack?'

He smiled. 'Yeah. Sure I am. Now get out of here, otherwise I'll have your beers drunk before you get back.'

***

Jack waited until Gwen had left before letting the smile slide off his face and into his water. His own loneliness ate a little deeper inside and he wondered if maybe he had a growing void inside him just like the one he'd glimpsed within the alien's screaming mouth. He wouldn't be surprised. Some kind of blackness was hardening at his core and he knew there was nothing he could do about it. It was the inescapable effect of his unusual life. Of the choices he had to make in his long, and seemingly endless existence.

Sighing, he drained what was left of the warm dregs of water that clung hopelessly to the inside of the bottle and felt them fizz into his chest. In a few hours, Detective Inspector Tom Cutler would wake up with a mild headache and all knowledge of Jack Harkness, Torchwood and Torchwood One would be wiped from his memory. The moment that defined his career and revealed so much about the strength of his character would be stripped from him and replaced with burning shame. But on the plus side, he'd also think he'd just solved Cardiff's most brutal serial killer case, and maybe that would go some way to allowing some self-absolution for long ago planting evidence on a guilty man in order to secure a conviction.

Tom Cutler's truth had changed. And maybe the new version might be easier to live with. The one thing Jack knew was that knowledge wasn't always good for the soul.

Watching the barman clean away Cutler's glass,

happily destroying any evidence of Retcon, Jack sighed. On the back bar, the front page of the *Western Mail* was filled with the image of Martin Meloy's weak face, his eyes staring balefully out, as if accusing Jack from beyond the grave. Martin Meloy's truth had changed too. Those who knew him would regale dinner parties for years to come with stories of how they always suspected 'there was something strange about him'. He'd never seemed 'quite right'. And then they'd tell tall tales of his macabre ways, invented so long ago that they'd believe them true themselves. The truth was like that: fluid and mercurial. There was maybe only one other person in the universe that understood that better than Jack, and he was a long way away, having adventures of his own.

Jack could use some time with him right now. He was a man who understood hard decisions and had a core of loneliness that probably beat Jack's own. Signalling the bartender, he thought of the alien and the singing boy, blended as one, probably far across the universe by now. He allowed himself a half-smile.

Some good had come out of this, even if the world would never know.

'A beer and a vodka diet coke, please.' He paused. 'And a brandy for me. Neat.'

Gwen and Ianto would be back soon and they'd raise his spirits with their own undaunted positivity. He was lucky to have them, lucky to have found them and he needed to keep hold of these good times, even if they threatened to be fleeting. One day, he'd need their memory and he couldn't waste the joy of the present when it could be found.

Because this was the twenty-first century. When everything would change. And Captain Jack Harkness intended to be ready.

ACKNOWLEDGEMENTS

I'd like to thank the following people for their help with this book. Firstly, best buddy and fellow author Mark Morris for persuading me to have a go at *Torchwood*, my editor Steve Tribe for making the whole process painless, and Sam and Andy for letting me live in their Scottish hideaway while I wrote it. And I couldn't go without thanking Jimmy George for his constant and boundless enthusiasm for all things *Doctor Who/Torchwood*-related!

TORCHWOOD
THE ENCYCLOPEDIA

ISBN 978 1 846 07764 7
£14.99

Founded by Queen Victoria in 1879, the Torchwood Institute has been defending Great Britain from the alien hordes for 130 years. Though London's Torchwood One was destroyed during the Battle of Canary Wharf, the small team at Torchwood Three have continued to monitor the space-time Rift that runs through Cardiff, saving the world and battling for the future of the human race.

Now you can discover every fact and figure, explore every crack in time and encounter every creature that Torchwood have dealt with. Included here are details of:

- The secret of the Children of Earth

- Operatives from Alice Guppy to Gwen Cooper

- Extraterrestrial visitors from Arcateenians to Weevils

- The life and deaths of Captain Jack Harkness

and much more. Illustrated throughout with photos and artwork from all three series, this A–Z provides everything you need to know about Torchwood.

Based on the hit series created by Russell T Davies for BBC Television.

Also available from BBC Books

TORCHWOOD
ANOTHER LIFE
Peter Anghelides

ISBN 978 0 563 48653 4
£6.99

Thick black clouds are blotting out the skies over Cardiff. As twenty-four inches of rain fall in twenty-four hours, the city centre's drainage system collapses. The capital's homeless are being murdered, their mutilated bodies left lying in the soaked streets around the Blaidd Drwg nuclear facility.

Tracked down by Torchwood, the killer calmly drops eight storeys to his death. But the killings don't stop. Their investigations lead Jack Harkness, Gwen Cooper and Toshiko Sato to a monster in a bathroom, a mystery at an army base and a hunt for stolen nuclear fuel rods. Meanwhile, Owen Harper goes missing from the Hub, when a game in *Second Reality* leads him to an old girlfriend…

Something is coming, forcing its way through the Rift, straight into Cardiff Bay.

Featuring Captain Jack Harkness as played by John Barrowman, with Gwen Cooper, Owen Harper, Toshiko Sato and Ianto Jones as played by Eve Myles, Burn Gorman, Naoki Mori and Gareth David-Lloyd, in the hit series created by Russell T Davies for BBC Television.

Also available from BBC Books

TORCHWOOD
BORDER PRINCES
Dan Abnett

ISBN 978 0 563 48654 1
£6.99

The End of the World began on a Thursday night in October,
just after eight in the evening…

The Amok is driving people out of their minds, turning them
into zombies and causing riots in the streets. A solitary diner
leaves a Cardiff restaurant, his mission to protect the Principal
leading him to a secret base beneath a water tower. Everyone
has a headache, there's something in Davey Morgan's shed,
and the church of St Mary-in-the-Dust, demolished in 1840,
has reappeared – though it's not due until 2011. Torchwood
seem to be out of their depth. What will all this mean for the
romance between Torchwood's newest members?

Captain Jack Harkness has something more to worry
about: an alarm, an early warning, given to mankind and held
– inert – by Torchwood for 108 years. And now it's flashing.
Something is coming. Or something is already here.

*Featuring Captain Jack Harkness as played by John Barrowman, with
Gwen Cooper, Owen Harper, Toshiko Sato and Ianto Jones as played by
Eve Myles, Burn Gorman, Naoki Mori and Gareth David-Lloyd, in the
hit series created by Russell T Davies for BBC Television.*

Also available from BBC Books

TORCHWOOD
SLOW DECAY
Andy Lane

ISBN 978 0 563 48655 8
£6.99

When Torchwood track an energy surge to a Cardiff nightclub, the team finds the police are already at the scene. Five teenagers have died in a fight, and lying among the bodies is an unfamiliar device. Next morning, they discover the corpse of a Weevil, its face and neck eaten away, seemingly by human teeth. And on the streets of Cardiff, an ordinary woman with an extraordinary hunger is attacking people and eating her victims.

The job of a lifetime it might be, but working for Torchwood is putting big strains on Gwen's relationship with Rhys. While she decides to spice up their love life with the help of alien technology, Rhys decides it's time to sort himself out – better music, healthier food, lose some weight. Luckily, a friend has mentioned Doctor Scotus's weight-loss clinic…

Featuring Captain Jack Harkness as played by John Barrowman, with Gwen Cooper, Owen Harper, Toshiko Sato and Ianto Jones as played by Eve Myles, Burn Gorman, Naoki Mori and Gareth David-Lloyd, in the hit series created by Russell T Davies for BBC Television.

TORCHWOOD
SOMETHING IN THE WATER
Trevor Baxendale

ISBN 978 1 84607 437 0
£6.99

Dr Bob Strong's GP surgery has been treating a lot of coughs and colds recently, far more than is normal for the time of year. Bob thinks there's something up but he can't think what. He seems to have caught it himself, whatever it is – he's starting to cough badly and there are flecks of blood in his hanky.

Saskia Harden has been found on a number of occasions submerged in ponds or canals but alive and seemingly none the worse for wear. Saskia is not on any files, except in the medical records at Dr Strong's GP practice.

But Torchwood's priorities lie elsewhere: investigating ghostly apparitions in South Wales, they have found a dead body. It's old and in an advanced state of decay. And it is still able to talk.

And what it is saying is 'Water hag'…

Featuring Captain Jack Harkness as played by John Barrowman, with Gwen Cooper, Owen Harper, Toshiko Sato and Ianto Jones as played by Eve Myles, Burn Gorman, Naoki Mori and Gareth David-Lloyd, in the hit series created by Russell T Davies for BBC Television.

TORCHWOOD
TRACE MEMORY
David Llewellyn

ISBN 978 1 84607 438 7
£6.99

Tiger Bay, Cardiff, 1953. A mysterious crate is brought into the docks on a Scandinavian cargo ship. Its destination: the Torchwood Institute. As the crate is offloaded by a group of local dockers, it explodes, killing all but one of them, a young Butetown lad called Michael Bellini.

Fifty-five years later, a radioactive source somewhere inside the Hub leads Torchwood to discover the same Michael Bellini, still young and dressed in his 1950s clothes, cowering in the vaults. They soon realise that each has encountered Michael before – as a child in Osaka, as a junior doctor, as a young police constable, as a new recruit to Torchwood One. But it's Jack who remembers him best of all.

Michael's involuntary time-travelling has something to do with a radiation-charged relic held inside the crate. And the Men in Bowler Hats are coming to get it back.

Featuring Captain Jack Harkness as played by John Barrowman, with Gwen Cooper, Owen Harper, Toshiko Sato and Ianto Jones as played by Eve Myles, Burn Gorman, Naoki Mori and Gareth David-Lloyd, in the hit series created by Russell T Davies for BBC Television.

Also available from BBC Books

TORCHWOOD

THE TWILIGHT STREETS
Gary Russell

ISBN 978 1 846 07439 4
£6.99

There's a part of the city that no one much goes to, a collection of rundown old houses and gloomy streets. No one stays there long, and no one can explain why – something's not quite right there.

Now the Council is renovating the district, and a new company is overseeing the work. There will be street parties and events to show off the newly gentrified neighbourhood: clowns and face-painters for the kids, magicians for the adults – the street entertainers of Cardiff, out in force.

None of this is Torchwood's problem. Until Toshiko recognises the sponsor of the street parties: Bilis Manger.

Now there is something for Torchwood to investigate. But Captain Jack Harkness has never been able to get into the area; it makes him physically ill to go near it. Without Jack's help, Torchwood must face the darker side of urban Cardiff alone...

Featuring Captain Jack Harkness as played by John Barrowman, with Gwen Cooper, Owen Harper, Toshiko Sato and Ianto Jones as played by Eve Myles, Burn Gorman, Naoki Mori and Gareth David-Lloyd, in the hit series created by Russell T Davies for BBC Television.

Also available from BBC Books

TORCHWOOD
PACK ANIMALS
Peter Anghelides

ISBN 978 1 846 07574 2
£6.99

Shopping for wedding gifts is enjoyable, unless like Gwen you witness a Weevil massacre in the shopping centre. A trip to the zoo is a great day out, until a date goes tragically wrong and Ianto is badly injured by stolen alien tech. And Halloween is a day of fun and frights, before unspeakable monsters invade the streets of Cardiff and it's no longer a trick or a treat for the terrified population.

Torchwood can control small groups of scavengers, but now someone has given large numbers of predators a season ticket to Earth. Jack's investigation is hampered when he finds he's being investigated himself. Owen is convinced that it's just one guy who's toying with them. But will Torchwood find out before it's too late that the game is horribly real, and the deck is stacked against them?

Featuring Captain Jack Harkness as played by John Barrowman, with Gwen Cooper, Owen Harper, Toshiko Sato and Ianto Jones as played by Eve Myles, Burn Gorman, Naoki Mori and Gareth David-Lloyd, in the hit series created by Russell T Davies for BBC Television.

TORCHWOOD
SKYPOINT
Phil Ford

ISBN 978 1 846 07575 9
£6.99

'If you're going to be anyone in Cardiff, you're going to be at SkyPoint!'

SkyPoint is the latest high-rise addition to the ever-developing Cardiff skyline. It's the most high-tech, avant-garde apartment block in the city. And it's where Rhys Williams is hoping to find a new home for himself and Gwen. Gwen's more concerned by the money behind the tower block – Besnik Lucca, a name she knows from her days in uniform.

When Torchwood discover that residents have been going missing from the tower block, one of the team gets her dream assignment. Soon SkyPoint's latest newly married tenants are moving in. And Toshiko Sato finally gets to make a home with Owen Harper.

Then something comes out of the wall…

Featuring Captain Jack Harkness as played by John Barrowman, with Gwen Cooper, Owen Harper, Toshiko Sato and Ianto Jones as played by Eve Myles, Burn Gorman, Naoki Mori and Gareth David-Lloyd, in the hit series created by Russell T Davies for BBC Television.

TORCHWOOD
ALMOST PERFECT
James Goss

ISBN 978 1 846 07573 5
£6.99

Emma is 30, single and frankly desperate. She woke up this morning with nothing to look forward to but another evening of unsuccessful speed-dating. But now she has a new weapon in her quest for Mr Right. And it's made her almost perfect.

Gwen Cooper woke up this morning expecting the unexpected. As usual. She went to work and found a skeleton at a table for two and a colleague in a surprisingly glamorous dress. Perfect.

Ianto Jones woke up this morning with no memory of last night. He went to work, where he caused amusement, suspicion and a little bit of jealousy. Because Ianto Jones woke up this morning in the body of a woman. And he's looking just about perfect.

Jack Harkness has always had his doubts about Perfection.

Featuring Captain Jack Harkness as played by John Barrowman, with Gwen Cooper and Ianto Jones as played by Eve Myles and Gareth David-Lloyd, in the hit series created by Russell T Davies for BBC Television.

TORCHWOOD
BAY OF THE DEAD
Mark Morris

ISBN 978 1 846 07737 1
£6.99

When the city sleeps, the dead start to walk…

Something has sealed off Cardiff, and living corpses are stalking the streets, leaving a trail of half-eaten bodies. Animals are butchered. A young couple in their car never reach their home. A stolen yacht is brought back to shore, carrying only human remains. And a couple of girls heading back from the pub watch the mysterious drivers of a big black SUV take over a crime scene.

Torchwood have to deal with the intangible barrier surrounding Cardiff, and some unidentified space debris that seems to be regenerating itself. Plus, of course, the all-night zombie horror show.

Not that they really believe in zombies.

Featuring Captain Jack Harkness as played by John Barrowman, with Gwen Cooper and Ianto Jones as played by Eve Myles and Gareth David-Lloyd, in the hit series created by Russell T Davies for BBC Television.

Coming soon from BBC Books

TORCHWOOD
THE UNDERTAKER'S GIFT
Trevor Baxendale

ISBN 978 1 846 07782 1
£6.99

The Hokrala Corp lawyers are back. They're suing planet Earth for mishandling the twenty-first century, and they won't tolerate any efforts to repel them. An assassin has been sent to remove Captain Jack Harkness.

It's been a busy week in Cardiff. The Hub's latest guest is a translucent, amber jelly carrying a lethal electrical charge. Record numbers of aliens have been coming through the Rift, and Torchwood could do without any more problems.

But there are reports of an extraordinary funeral cortege in the night-time city, with mysterious pallbearers guarding a rotting cadaver that simply doesn't want to be buried.

Torchwood should be ready for anything – but with Jack the target of an invisible killer, Gwen trapped in a forgotten crypt and Ianto Jones falling desperately ill, could a world of suffering be the Undertaker's gift to planet Earth?

Featuring Captain Jack Harkness as played by John Barrowman, with Gwen Cooper and Ianto Jones as played by Eve Myles and Gareth David-Lloyd, in the hit series created by Russell T Davies for BBC Television.

TORCHWOOD
RISK ASSESSMENT
James Goss

ISBN 978 1 846 07783 8
£6.99

'Are you trying to tell me, Captain Harkness, that the entire staff of Torchwood Cardiff now consists of yourself, a woman in trousers and a tea boy?'

Agnes Haversham is awake, and Jack is worried (and not a little afraid). The Torchwood Assessor is roused from her deep sleep in only the worst of times – it's happened just four times in the last 100 years. Can the situation really be so bad?

Someone, somewhere, is fighting a war, and they're losing badly. The coffins of the dead are coming through the Rift. With thousands of alien bodies floating in the Bristol Channel, it's down to Torchwood to round them all up before a lethal plague breaks out.

And now they'll have to do it by the book. The 1901 edition.

Featuring Captain Jack Harkness as played by John Barrowman, with Gwen Cooper and Ianto Jones as played by Eve Myles and Gareth David-Lloyd, in the hit series created by Russell T Davies for BBC Television.

TORCHWOOD
CONSEQUENCES

ISBN 978 1 846 07784 5

£6.99

Saving the planet, watching over the Rift, preparing the human race for the twenty-first century... Torchwood has been keeping Cardiff safe since the late 1800s. Small teams of heroes, working 24/7, encountering and containing the alien, the bizarre and the inexplicable.

But Torchwood do not always see the effects of their actions. What links the Rules and Regulations for replacing a Torchwood leader to the destruction of a shopping centre? How does a witness to an alien's reprisals against Torchwood become caught up in a night of terror in a university library? And why should Gwen and Ianto's actions at a local publishers have a cost for Torchwood more than half a century earlier?

For Torchwood, the past will always catch up with them. And sometimes the future will catch up with the past...

Featuring stories by writers for the hit series created by Russell T Davies for BBC Television, including Joseph Lidster and James Moran, plus Andrew Cartmel, David Llewellyn and Sarah Pinborough.